The Black Daiquiri

An Arrow Investigations Mystery

KC Walker

Acknowledgments

My gorgeous cover was designed by Mariah Sinclair, aka the Cozy Queen. Find her at https://www.thecov ervault.com or on Facebook.

Thanks to the 1667 Club for the moral support and especially for the laughs!

To my wonderful readers. You give me inspiration, ideas, moral support, and encouragement (and find the most persistent of typos!). You are what makes all the hard work worthwhile.

To Kit

You came into my life just when I needed you.

This book is dedicated to you and all the dogs with mysterious and tragic backstories. I'm grateful to be a part of your Happy Ever After.

Chapter One

I crouched behind the office door, bracing for the attack. The tattooed man entered the room, menace in his eyes and a knife in his hand. I leapt, twisted in the air, and kicked the weapon from his hand.

No time for a pat on the back just yet. Four more attackers surged into the room, ready to finish me off. Where do you run when you're on the tenth floor and the bad guys are blocking the exit?

I took off full speed toward the window, turning as I crashed through so I wouldn't cut my face.

"Cut," the director called.

I landed on the mattress and brushed the sugar glass off my spandex catsuit.

He leaned through the window frame and gave me a smarmy smile. "Great job, Whitley."

"Thanks! Does that mean it's the last take?"

"Sure does, babe," he said. "You're done unless we have any reshoots."

When he'd first taken over as director, I'd complained about him calling women "babe" and "sweetie," but was told that was just how the older generation talked. I was also told not to make waves.

I came around the set onto the stage. "Hope we get to work together again." It didn't hurt to brownnose a little, especially if it got me more work. Now that the show had been canceled, I'd be looking for another job.

In the excitement of finishing my final scene, I forgot about the director's nickname: Mr. Handsy.

As I walked past him, he grabbed my butt cheek and gave it a squeeze. Years of training kicked in before my brain did, and before I knew it, he was lying on his back on the floor, gasping.

His face reddened and his nostrils flared as he tried to catch his breath. I must have knocked the wind out of him.

"You," he finally managed to say, pointing a shaky finger at me. "What's wrong with you?"

"Don't ever touch me again," I said.

He slowly climbed to his feet. "You're crazy. I want you off my set now."

"Gladly." I headed toward the dressing rooms.

"Did you see what she did?" he bellowed to the

few people still on set. "Get that crazy bitch out of here."

The room had gone silent as everyone watched the show. The assistant director, a boyish and eager young man in a polo shirt, headed my way.

"Why do you let him get away with it?" I asked him as he escorted me to the dressing rooms.

"I need to keep my job," he said. "We all do. Don't ruin it for the rest of us."

"The rest of us? You mean the men? I'm pretty sure he's already ruined it for the women."

Had anyone seen the director grab my butt before I flipped him? I had a sinking feeling that even if they had, they wouldn't stick out their necks to help out a lowly stunt double they hardly knew.

◈ ⇢⇉

Six Months Later

I walked right past the Hotel Elegance and had to double back. As many times as I'd visited my parents' nearby beach cottage, I'd never paid much attention to the hotel. Its Spanish Colonial architecture blended in with the newer shops and businesses facing the street.

The reflection of a dark-haired woman in the

window startled me before I recognized myself. I'd just chopped most of my hair off, tired of bleaching it blonde to look like the actress I doubled for. I ran my fingers through the thick mane in a fruitless attempt to tame it.

"Stop fussing," I told myself.

The moment I stepped inside the hotel, its age and authenticity became apparent with its white stucco walls, arched doorways, and worn oak floor. To the left was a fireplace with a huge wooden mantel. Through a pair of glass doors to the right I spotted a restaurant, though that might have been overselling the tiny space.

Toward the back of the lobby stood a reception counter, just wide enough that two very thin supermodels might have fit behind it. Possibly supermodels were not available, so they had settled for one plump, freckle-faced brunette.

"Welcome to Hotel Elegance and Spa," the young woman said by way of a greeting. "My name is Courtney."

The lobby didn't give me the same freshly scrubbed vibe as Courtney. From the seventies-era rugs, worn thin in high-traffic areas, to the dim lighting, the place appeared in need of a refresh or maybe a total remodel. I didn't see any sign of a spa, but maybe they had it hidden away with the elegance, which was in short supply.

Courtney watched me, no doubt waiting for me to return her greeting.

"Hi." I hoped that was enough pleasantries. "I'm here to see Bat. Bat Keller."

"Oh." She seemed disappointed I hadn't stopped in for a nice, long chat. "He's up on the roof."

"The roof? What's he doing on the roof?"

She brightened, possibly hoping this was the beginning of our chat. "Oh, you've never been to our rooftop lounge? The view up there is lovely."

"Thanks." I headed for the stairs, taking them two at a time.

She called after me. "There's an elevator."

Three flights of stairs later, I emerged into the bright sunlight. I pulled my Ray-bans down from on top of my head and scoped out the place. Hotel Elegance's rooftop lounge seemed like the perfect place to grab a cold drink and kick back.

A few men sat at the bar day drinking. Most of the tables were taken by groups lingering over their lunches as they soaked up the rays, the view, and their martinis, not necessarily in that order. A group of well-dressed women with huge designer sunglasses shrieked with laughter, a sign it was time to call them a cab.

My gaze focused on what was on the other side of the bar--a very hot bartender. The customers got a spectacular view of the ocean, complete with sailboats and offshore oil platforms, but with his back to the water, all he got to look at was middle-aged drunks. Of course, there were plenty of beautiful women that would come to a place like this, but probably not alone.

I found an empty spot at the bar and waited for the bartender to acknowledge me, which didn't take long.

"What can I get you?" he asked in a low, bedroom voice with just a touch of gravel.

"I'm here to see Bat Keller."

He squinted as if the sun was in his eyes, but it was high above us. "Why do you want to see him?"

"Why don't you just let him know I'm asking for him. You can tell him Whitley Leland is here." A little attitude might have slipped into my voice.

The hot bartender laughed. I narrowed my eyes the way I did when I wanted to intimidate someone. He better not laugh at me, even if he did look like a young Ryan Reynolds—if Ryan Reynolds had dark hair and blue eyes that could melt your panties right off your body. Come to think of it, he looked nothing like Ryan Reynolds.

He reached out a hand. "I'm Bat."

I shook his hand. If he expected me to act embarrassed or apologize, he had the wrong woman. I'd done way more embarrassing things in my day. If he didn't want to hire me, there were plenty of jobs for out-of-work stunt performers. I didn't know what they were, but I was pretty sure I would be in high demand once the word got out that I was available.

"Here I am. As promised. Your new bouncer."

He squinted again. Did the guy have an astigmatism? "Bouncer slash bartender."

"Huh?" I squinted back. "What's with the slash? Does everyone within two hundred miles of L.A. have to have a slash in their job title? What are you—a bartender slash manager?"

Bat smiled at my rant. "I'm a bartender slash owner of this fine establishment."

"You own this bar?" I asked.

"I own this hotel."

"Hotel slash spa," I corrected.

He ignored my little joke. "Have you ever tended bar?"

"Nope." I set my elbows on the bar the way my mother taught me not to. "I know exactly what side of the bar I belong on, and it's this side. You know, the side where I drink the fancy, expensive cocktails that the bartender shakes up in his, um, shaker. Trent said you needed someone who could handle rowdy customers, and while I'm waiting for my next gig, I thought it wouldn't hurt to come meet with you."

"How do you know Trent anyway?" he asked.

"He's an associate producer on the *Legends of the Defenders*. I've been a stunt double on that show since the first season. Do you watch it?"

"I watched the first season or two. Is it still on?"

I'd heard that question too many times. "Just got canceled. Apparently, the viewership kept dropping every season." With so many shows to watch, people had forgotten our series was still on the air.

"How long have you been out of work?"

"I'm on a hiatus." 'Out of work,' sounded so desperate.

"Okay." A smile played on his lips. "How long have you been on *hiatus* then."

I wondered how much this guy knew about my past. Did he think he was doing me a favor by offering me a job? "When a long-running series ends, it always takes a while to get on another show. People tend to forget about you."

"Trent got another job right away."

"Yeah, well." I didn't want to share the real reason my calls and texts weren't being returned. "It's complicated."

Bat reached for his shiny, silver cocktail shaker and removed the top. "As long as you're here, why don't I fix you one of those fancy, expensive cocktails." He scooped some ice and rattled it around teasingly. I don't know how you rattle ice teasingly, but that's what Bat did. "On the house."

"Sure, why not." I might as well get a free drink out of this wasted attempt to find meaningful employment. "You know, I'm a really good bouncer." I'd never actually been a bouncer, but some things you just know.

"I'm sure you are." He poured what appeared to be random bottles of liquor into the shaker along with a few shots of colored liquid from plastic bottles with handwritten labels. "I like a bouncer who doesn't look like a bouncer. When you have one of those big beefy guys with his tight, black t-shirt, people expect trouble. And when people come into my hotel and drink at my rooftop lounge, I want them to relax and spend lots of money."

"So why can't I just be a bouncer slash bouncer?"

"Listen, unlike Trent and the rest of your studio friends in L.A., I'm not made of money. I don't have the budget for a bouncer, a hostess, a couple of bartenders, a cabana boy, and a—"

"You have a pool?" Now he had my attention. A cabana boy would be nice too.

"Not unless you count the hot tub in the spa." Bat poured his concoction into a martini glass, adding a fancy cherry which sank to the bottom.

"There really is a spa?" I asked. "Is Courtney a front desk clerk slash masseuse?"

"She's a front desk clerk slash my sister." He

placed the drink in front of me. "Let me know what you think."

"What is it?" I eyed the dark, evil-looking drink suspiciously.

"An Elegance Black Daiquiri."

"Oh, I get it. Is this one of your signature drinks? I bet the girly-girls lap these up."

He sucked in a breath and huffed, "It won't kill you."

The inky, purple concoction *looked* like something that would kill me. I took a tentative sip and felt my tastebuds wake up. After the second sip, they did a little dance. My lips started to turn up at the corners in what might be considered a smile.

"Admit it. That's the best thing you've tasted in a long time."

"How would you know what I've tasted?" That sounded like a bad come-on line, so I clarified. "I'll have you know I've been to some of the finest bars in town."

"Drink up and I'll make you another, and this time I'll teach you how to make it."

"Good idea," I said. "That way I can make it at home and save my money."

Bat lifted the pass-through and waited for me to come around to his side of the bar. "On second thought, let's start with something simpler. How about a lemon drop?"

"Now we're talking. Bobbie—that's my grandmother--loves those. I can get her drunk next time I go see her."

Bat seemed concerned, probably thinking that Bobbie was a sweet, little old lady who needed protection from her wayward granddaughter, which couldn't be further from the truth.

"You start with what we call a mixing glass," he said, setting a glass tumbler on the bar.

"Who thought up that name?"

He ignored my question. "Toss in a sugar cube." He dropped one into the glass, and it made a tiny ping.

"Why not simple syrup?" He was about to find out that I ask a lot of questions. And I mean, a lot.

Bat raised his eyebrows, a sure sign he was about to dispense some bartender wisdom. "Do you think simple syrup would make that sound when it hit the glass?"

"Ah," I said appreciatively. "You give them a bit of show with the drink." I paused for just a moment before adding, "And by a bit, I mean a teeny tiny bit."

He ignored my comment. "Add lemon juice and muddle the sugar cube." He took a wooden stick and jammed it in the glass, crushing the defenseless sugar. It was very manly.

"Our signature lemon drop is made with Ketel One vodka and limoncello." He showed me the rest of the steps, shook it over ice, and poured it into a martini glass with a sugared rim.

"Very nice," I said and took a sip. "Man, that's good."

"Make sure you confirm that the customer wants a Signature Lemon Drop."

"Got it," I said with a firm nod. "Is someone going to be upset if they get the good vodka?"

"No, but they might be upset when you charge them eighteen dollars."

"Eighteen dollars?" I nearly spit out my drink. "I'm in trouble if I get used to this and can't drink the cheap stuff anymore."

"You won't be in any trouble," he assured me. "You get to drink free. After your shift, of course."

"I don't think I'd make a very good bartender," I said, wanting to keep my options open. "I'd make a badass bouncer, though."

After shaking the drink vigorously, I poured it into a martini glass and took a sip. "Man, that's good. I always knew I'd be a great bartender, if I wanted to be a bartender, which I don't."

Slipping out from behind the bar, I returned to my stool and watched as the bar slowly filled up with locals and tourists pretending to be locals. They didn't fool me—no self-respecting beach resident would iron their Hawaiian shirts and Bermuda shorts.

Between the warm October sun and the rhythmic sound of the waves three floors below, my tense shoulders began to relax. The cool, salty, ocean breeze didn't hurt either, not to mention the lemon drop.

After an hour of sipping cocktails and chatting with Bat the Charmer, I walked down the three flights of stairs to the Hotel Elegance lobby with a plastic, spiral-bound recipe book and a buzz.

"Hello, again," Courtney greeted me as if I were an old friend. "How'd it go?"

"I'm not sure," I answered.

"Oh, I'm sorry," she said. "Bat didn't hire you?"

"Actually, he did."

Courtney came running out from behind her counter with her arms outstretched. "Congratulations!"

"Whoa." I threw my arms up to stop her. "I don't do hugs." When I saw her disappointment, I suggested, "Celebratory fist bump?"

She grinned and held out her fist. "Nice to have you as part of our family."

I gave her fist a quick tap. As I headed out the front door, I muttered to myself, "As if one family isn't more than enough."

Heading south, I made my way to my temporary home. I had a sweet setup at my parents' beach cottage, one of three family homes... or was it four? I might have lost count. My parents lived in Beverly Hills most of the year.

I had been offered it "no strings attached," but I knew from experience that there would be enough string to wrap me up like a cocoon before I could get back to L.A. That would happen as soon as I got another studio gig and found a new place to live.

Since it was only four in the afternoon, I put on a pot of coffee to brew to clear my head, not to mention sober up. I carried the cocktail recipe handbook out to the patio where I had about two hours of sunshine to enjoy before dusk.

Joggers, bicyclists, and the occasional rollerblader whizzed by on the path that separated our patio and the sand. I'd have to get back to running or risk getting out of shape.

In my line of work, I had to be in tip top form at all times. One of the patio chairs got stuck on a table leg, so I gave it a yank. The chair came loose and sent me flying backwards. Luckily the chaise lounge broke my fall.

Regaining my composure, I uprighted the chair and myself. Opening the handbook, I read Bat's notes on which brands to offer to upsell the customer. What a racket. I used all my memorization tricks, from copying down all the recipes in a notebook to using mnemonics so I could remember ingredients. When my eyes started to cross, I turned on my laptop and watched YouTube videos. There were a lot of sexy looking men and women making drinks for my entertainment and edification.

I fell asleep on the sofa and dreamt of Bat, shirtless, making me a Black Daiquiri.

Chapter Two

On my first day at work, I showed up in a white shirt as instructed. It was Valentino, and my mother would kill me if she found out I'd been in her closet, but I'd worry about that later.

Bat quizzed me on increasingly obscure drink recipes, and I nailed them all, one after the other.

He stopped me as I recited the ingredients for a Blue Lagoon. "What did you just say?'

"Cure a cow," I repeated.

Bat thought this was hilarious. I waited for him to stop laughing, which took a while.

"It's Curaçao," he corrected. "The first "C" is hard, like your head, and the second "C" is soft."

"Soft like your head?" I gave him a playful grin.

"Pretty impressive, even with the cow remedy. I

had a feeling you'd catch on quickly." He walked over to the end of the bar and retrieved a vest and an apron. He handed them to me.

"Oh, thanks," I said. "I don't really do vests." The look he gave me made me reconsider my reply, so I added, "Until now. Very stylish."

"The white shirt is mandatory, but you can wear a black skirt or leggings." He eyed my jeans. "Or those. Do you have a newer pair that's less gray and more...black?"

"I have about twenty pairs of black jeans. I'll make sure to wear my nicest ones, just for you."

He ignored my fawning smile. "I recommend comfortable shoes. Black, of course." He gave my black combat boots a disapproving look.

"These have gotten me through a lot." They'd have to do, since my mother and I wore different shoe sizes.

He sighed. "Fine. For now. Maybe you can use part of your first paycheck to get something more professional."

"Oh sure. Now can I practice jumping over the bar?" I'd been waiting for the chance.

Bat stared at me. "What makes you think you'll need to do that?"

"Bouncers always do that when there's a ruckus."

"We don't have—" he shook his head, as if trying to think of the plural of ruckus. "The lounge is chill most of the time. I just need someone who can watch the bar when I'm not around—someone who won't be intimidated by some random dude giving them a hard time."

He must have seen the look of disappointment on my face. I'd had an actor roommate once who showed me how to cry on demand. I blinked a couple of times as if holding back tears. It might have actually worked.

"Fine. You can jump over the bar just once."

"Yay!" I didn't wait for him to change his mind. I ran a couple of steps to get some momentum, placed both hands on the bar and swung my legs over, nailing the landing just as a leggy blonde emerged from the elevator.

The blonde gave me a disapproving shake of her head as if I were an unruly toddler.

"Ta-da," I said hopefully, my hands held out to my side the way I'd learned as a gymnast.

Bat slipped out from behind the bar and gave the woman a kiss on the cheek. "This is the new bartender I was telling you about."

In response, she raised her eyebrows only slightly, no doubt hindered by Botox.

"Whit," he went on, "This is my fiancée, Deborah."

Fiancée? Despite my disappointment, I gave her a friendly smile and said, "Nice to meet you." I returned to my post behind the bar so they could be alone, and so I didn't have to look at the perfect display of femininity who was planning to marry Bat. Not that I wanted to marry the guy, but I wouldn't have minded taking him for a test drive before he got all serious with someone else. Maybe it was better this way, or at least that's what I told myself. Besides, I always had Dream Bat.

After Deborah left, the rest of the night flew by, as I avoided comparing myself to Bat's blonde bombshell. I remembered every recipe, but making the drinks was another thing. Turns out book learning and real-life experience were two different things. Who knew?

Bat showed me some tricks of the trade, and I asked questions. Some of them were pertinent, some not, but there was one thing I wanted to know.

"How did you get the name Bat?" I asked, as I sugared the rim of a martini glass for a Sidecar. "Were you named after the flying, bug-eating mammals, or were your parents baseball fans?"

"Never scoop ice with the glass," he said, when he caught me doing just that. "Always use the tool intended for that purpose." He held up the ice scoop. "If the glass breaks, we have to 86 the whole bin, and that's not something you want to do in the middle of a rush."

"86?"

"Dump it. We use the term for patrons too if they're no longer welcome."

"Got it," I assured him. "And how'd you get your name?"

He sighed, seemingly tired of telling the story. "It's short for Bartholomew. I was named after my grandfather. Courtney couldn't say Bart, so she called me Bat, and it stuck."

"Your name is Bartholomew?"

He narrowed his eyes. "No one, and I mean no one, calls me that."

"I saw that name on a picture in the lobby. Is that your grandfather?"

"My great-grandfather," Bat said. "He built the hotel in 1929, and it's been in the family ever since. I've been going through the process to have it declared a historical landmark since my grandfather passed away last year. That's the only way to protect it from being torn down."

"How could someone tear it down if it's your hotel?"

"They can't, unless they buy it." He set his jaw firmly. "And I'm not about to sell."

Chapter Three

The next morning, my feet hurt so badly I could barely stand. After hitting every shoe store in town, I learned a hard lesson. Comfortable shoes are either very ugly or very expensive. Usually both.

A pair of black running shoes would have worked, but none of the stores in town carried my favorite brand. After an encounter with a persuasive salesperson, I blew fifty bucks on a pair of cushy insoles to slip inside my boots.

Instead of walking eight blocks to work, I drove to save the wear and tear on my feet. When I realized I'd have to park six blocks away, I turned the car around and went back home. I wore my running shoes for the walk and carried my boots in a tote.

My shift started at four, the same time as happy

hour. The lounge was hopping by the time I'd changed shoes and slipped behind the bar.

Bat leaned close and whispered. "Tonight, I'm gonna let you work the bar, and I'll be your backup if you get busy."

"Or if I have questions?"

He walked away without answering, almost as if he didn't appreciate my quest for knowledge.

By the end of the night, I figured I could handle the bar by myself on a slow night, if I didn't get too many orders for specialty cocktails. Bat didn't appreciate my suggestion for premixed cocktails at all.

I soon concluded the lounge did not have any slow nights. But as long as I had Bat to come to my rescue, we'd be fine.

"Do you ever take a day off?" I asked.

"I used to take Mondays and Tuesdays off when we were fully staffed, but it's been tough finding good people lately."

"Lucky for you I came along when I did, then."

As a quick learner, I leaned on my strengths. Turned out, I excelled at being rude to customers and making them think I was being funny.

I'd also become an expert at leaning against the wall when Bat wasn't looking. Those "comfort" inserts I'd put in my boots were nearly useless, but I hoped having the next two days off would help.

At the end of the night, I had a wad of tip money

to get me through until payday. As I walked home past closed shops and restaurants, my weariness grew with each step. There was no way I was going anywhere on my days off unless they offered foot massages.

The next morning, coffee mug in hand, I hobbled out to the patio overlooking the sand and the sea. A cool, briny breeze swept over me as a flock of seagulls squawked overhead. The few joggers passing by reminded me of my resolution to stay in shape, but my feet hurt too much to go running.

I stretched out on the chaise lounge and emailed my favorite stunt coordinators to see what jobs were coming up. I got an evasive email back from one with a comment about my attitude. By now, I thought they'd remember the work I did and forget about my sassy personality.

"I'm a stunt person," I told myself. "Bartending is only temporary." For some reason, telling myself this only got me more depressed.

I spent the rest of the morning doing strength training—everything I'd learned to do without weights or equipment. If I stayed in town much longer, I'd have to break down and pay for a gym membership.

After making myself lunch, I went online looking for a secondhand store. One white blouse wasn't going to get me through the week, and I didn't want to spend my meager savings on something so mundane. After visiting two local shops, I scored an Egyptian cotton blouse. After much indecision, I bought another polyester blend shirt as a backup that I hoped I would never need to wear.

By the second day, boredom got the better of me. A run would do me a world of good, so I tested my sore feet on the soft sand. When they didn't protest, I took off north along the beach.

Several minutes later, I reached the stairs that led up a small cliff to Hotel Elegance. Viewing the hotel from the rear, all I could see of the rooftop lounge was the big blue umbrellas. Out of habit, I scoped out the building's exterior. Many times, I'd been on location and asked to climb up the side of a building, and I always found a way, even when others said it couldn't be done.

With one last look up the coast, I turned and headed home. Back at the cottage, my feet felt rejuvenated as if the sand had given them massage, and it didn't cost me a cent.

The next day, I slept in until nearly noon. After three cups of coffee, a bowl of cereal, and checking my emails seventeen times, I gave up on my job search for the time being and got ready for my shift.

I walked barefoot along the sand, carrying my boots. That worked fine until I hit the sidewalk, which burned like hot coals. I took off running, hoping to make it to the front door before my soles had blisters.

As I burst through the lobby door, Courtney

greeted me with a cheerful smile. "Do you need a towel to wipe the sand off your feet?"

"Good idea." Sand inside my socks would be annoying at best. "Man, that sidewalk is hot."

"Probably why most people wear shoes or sandals."

Was that sarcasm? From Courtney? Either way, I gave her a snarky, "Thanks for the tip."

She pulled a towel from behind her little counter and tossed it to me. "Would you wipe the sand off outside please?"

"Just what I had planned to do," I lied. "I wasn't born in a barn."

"I didn't mean—"

I held up a hand to stop her from apologizing. Somehow, I needed to figure out how to toughen her up a bit. Or perhaps I could learn to be gentler. I gave it a try. "Of course, you didn't mean anything." I grabbed the towel and stepped outside, hopping on one foot and then the other as I wiped off my feet.

Mostly sand-free, I took a seat in the lobby and put my shoes on while Courtney pretended not to watch me. I held out the towel. "Want me to wash this and bring it back?"

"Naw, I'll throw it in with the laundry. We're used to sand around here."

"Okay, well, see you later." I headed for the stairs.

When I emerged at the rooftop lounge, Bat

greeted me cheerfully. "Get ready for a busy night," he said, before he went to the storage room for more liquor bottles.

"Great," I said, leaning against the bar, standing on first one foot and then the other. I couldn't believe my feet still hurt after two days off.

"It'll get better, I promise," one of the servers said. "Two house whites, please."

"Coming right up." I grabbed two wine glasses. "Jenny, right?"

She nodded. "After the first week, your feet don't hurt so bad. Either that, or eventually you buy those lace-up orthopedic shoes and throw self-respect out the window."

"Ah, yes." I placed the drinks on the bar. "Let's hope it doesn't come to that."

Bat returned and chatted up a middle-aged man at the end of the bar who I took to be a regular, while I rinsed glasses and placed them to drain next to the sink.

As soon as Bat left to go check on something downstairs, the customer turned his attention to me. "So, gorgeous, are you a model?"

I managed not to roll my eyes. No one of normal height and size could get modeling gigs, assuming they wanted to keep their clothes on. I ignored him.

"Actor? Artist? I bet you're an artist. Lots of artists live around here."

"Do you want another martini?" I asked.

"Screenwriter!" he guessed. He must have seen me wince. "I knew it!"

"Yeah, I'm impressed you got it on the fourth try." It wasn't exactly a lie. Everybody in L.A. had a half-finished screenplay on their laptop, even me.

"Dumbass." This comment came from the opposite end of the bar.

"That better not be meant for me, Dolph," I warned. His name was Randolph, and I'm sure his friends called him Randy, but he liked to be called Dolph and I liked to be tipped, so that was settled. The patio lights reflected off his scalp despite his attempt at a combover.

"She's a stuntwoman," Dolph informed the curious martini drinker.

I made my way down the bar until I reached Dolph. I put my elbows on the bar and leaned as close as I could without giving him a view down my blouse. It would probably get me a better tip, but I didn't want him getting the wrong idea.

I spoke just loud enough for him to hear me. "If I wanted him to know that information, don't you think I would have mentioned it myself?"

"Sorry, hon," he began.

"Sorry, who?"

"Sorry, Whit." He stared at his drink sadly, as if he really wanted another but was afraid to ask.

Sometimes I forgot the effect I had on people when I neglected to smile and talk softly. But it was exhausting being nice twenty-four seven. That's why I liked my job--my stunt performer job. A stunt double just has to show up and kick butt and is hardly ever asked to smile and look pretty. That's the actor's job.

"Ready for another?" I forced myself to give him a kindly smile.

"I'll have another," the man Dolph had called a dumbass said. In my head, that would be his name from now on.

"I didn't ask you." I did my best to ignore Bat's glare as he slipped behind the bar.

"I'll make you another, Joe," Bat told the thirsty guy.

Darn. Now that I knew his name, I couldn't call him dumbass anymore. At least not to his face.

Bat pulled me aside, and I prepared myself for a scolding. "Joe is one of our best customers," he informed me. "He eats dinner here three or four times a week, and you might be interested in knowing that he tips very well."

"So, I should make nice with him?' I asked. "For money?"

"Just try not to be rude," he said, and returned to the other end of the bar.

"Whit is quite a handful," I overheard Joe tell Bat. "How do you manage to keep her in line?"

"I'm working on it."

An hour or so later, I turned to see Bat shaking his head. "How do you do it?"

"Do what?"

He handed me a twenty with a note attached. "For Whit," it said, and Joe had written his phone number down.

I stuffed the bill in my pocket and trashed the note. "What can I say? When you got it, you got it."

"You've got it all right. I just don't know what 'it' is."

Chapter Four

The lounge had quieted down from the dinner rush. The lull allowed us to restock and regroup before the late-night crowd showed up. Those limes didn't cut themselves into wedges.

Courtney slid onto a barstool and gave me a little wave. I hoped she wasn't looking for a new best friend. She seemed like the type that would want to go shopping together and do sleepovers where we'd put mud masks on our faces and braid each other's hair.

I set a beach-themed coaster in front of her. "Can I get you a drink?"

"Yes, please. I'd like a Black Daiquiri."

"Coming right up. They are quite delicious, I must admit, but a bit too potent for me."

"Oh," Courtney seemed embarrassed, as if I'd just called her a lush. "I can handle one, but no more."

"Yes, but the problem is, they're so dang yummy, I want at least three."

Courtney laughed. "You have a point there. After I drink this, don't let me order another, okay?"

The girl was so adorable and innocent, I'm sure it brought out the protective instinct in most people. I didn't want to be responsible for anyone but myself, so I resisted. "You need to take responsibility for yourself," I told her firmly.

Courtney seemed taken aback. "Of course. I was just making a joke."

Great. Now I'd hurt her feelings. Ticking people off was nothing new for me, but she was the boss's sister. "Yeah, me too," I lied. "Can't you take a joke?" I gave her a wink. It must have worked since her perky smile came back.

A dark-haired, thirty-ish man with a pasty complexion took off his leather jacket, sat on the stool next to her, and ordered a whiskey and soda. No fancy-schmancy drinks for him. Courtney seemed to know him, or maybe she'd seen him at the bar before, so I left them alone to talk. She was single, after all, and he was about the right age and moderately attractive, even if he could use some time in the sun.

Courtney left the bar to visit the ladies' room. I'd have to talk to her about leaving her drink unattended.

I'd gotten so many lectures from my mother on the subject, it was second nature to me.

This wasn't one of those meat-market types of nightclubs full of lonely, single people that might attract a predator. Despite that, and perhaps because of some deep-seated trust issues when it came to men, I kept an eye on Courtney's drink.

He was slick, I'll give him that. If I hadn't been watching and waiting to see what he would do, I probably never would have noticed him drop something in her drink.

Courtney returned to her seat and gave him a smile that made me so mad I wanted to jump over the bar and throw him off the roof. But as much fun as that would be for me, and as painful as it would be for him, he belonged in jail. And that was just where he was going.

All I had to do now was keep Courtney from drinking the daiquiri while not letting him know I was onto him. And while I was doing that, someone needed to call the police. Good thing I was an expert multitasker.

I took a few steps in their direction, trying to be nonchalant.

"Don't you like your drink?" he asked. "You've hardly touched it."

That was my cue. I stepped up to them and reached for her drink. "I'll make you something else." I grabbed the drink before she could stop me and put it below the bar. I would figure out how to get it tested later.

"Why'd you do that, Whit?" Courtney protested. "It was really good."

The man put a couple of bills on the bar, even though his drink was half full. "You're not leaving so soon, I hope," I said flirtatiously.

He made eye contact. I was never good at hiding my feelings, and he saw right through me. Without saying a word, he darted for the stairs.

"Come back," I yelled. There was no time to waste. Good thing I'd practiced jumping over the bar. I leapt over it, landing on the other side just as the elevator opened, releasing a group of older patrons that must have taken a wrong turn at the bingo hall. I tried to maneuver around them, but I knew by the time I made it to the lobby, he'd be long gone.

I yelled at Bat, "Call the cops!" then raced to the end of the lounge that overlooked the street below. Without thinking twice, I grabbed the railing and swung over the side. Scampering down the drainpipe, I climbed onto a second-floor balcony.

A woman inside stared with her mouth wide. I gave her a nod then leaned over the balcony railing to scope out the rest of my descent. A striped awning below appeared sturdy enough. I climbed over the side of the balcony and leapt onto the awning, bouncing a few times. Grabbing onto the edge, I swung down to the sidewalk.

With no time to waste, I ran to the main street just in time to see the man burst out of the front door. His mouth dropped open, but after a split-second of indecision, he ran off in the opposite direction. I could run five miles barely breaking a sweat, and I looked forward to finding out what kind of shape he was in. I forgot all about my sore feet as I took off. Adrenaline could do that.

He had almost a half-block lead on me. As I gained on him, he tried to ditch me by turning down one side street and up another. Then he turned into an alley.

I didn't see the gun until I was almost on top of him. Forget rock, paper, scissors. A gun wins every time.

I threw my arms up. "Hey, let's not get crazy. I just want to know why you put roofies in Courtney's drink."

He laughed. I think it was a laugh, but it was hard to tell between the huffing and puffing. If I had a gun, I might laugh, too. "You think I'm some kind of a perv?"

"Yes," I said. "That's exactly what I think."

"If you know what's good for you," he said, in between trying to catch his breath, "you'll forget you ever saw me."

Who wrote this guy's dialogue? "You watch too

many movies," I said. "You need to get out more. Get some exercise so you're not so winded after a long chase." To be fair, I was out of breath, too.

He looked at me dumbfounded. "Who are you?"

"Funny, I was about to ask you the same question."

Tires squealed, and a shiny, black sedan right out of central casting pulled up next to us, one of the back doors flying open. The perv jumped in and left me standing there.

Half expecting someone to yell "cut," I took off running. I know I can't run as fast as a car. I really do. Even so, I chased after it anyway, but after two blocks, I gave up. At least I got the plate number.

Walking back to Hotel Elegance took nearly twenty minutes, which meant I must have chased the guy for a mile. I took the elevator for a change, and as I stepped out onto the rooftop lounge, applause broke out.

Courtney ran over. "You jumped off the building."

"I remember."

"Why did you chase him?" she asked.

"Darn." Running man's drink was gone. A rocks glass sat on the drainer, freshly washed. I turned to Bat, who watched me curiously. "Was that his glass?"

Bat cocked his head to one side, not yet understanding what had almost just happened. "Was I supposed to save it?"

So much for getting the guy's fingerprints. I

slipped behind the bar and found Courtney's drink I'd stashed. At least Bat had left that alone. I found a nearly empty cherry jar, which I emptied and rinsed out before pouring an ounce or so of the doctored drink in it, leaving the rest for the cops. If anyone wondered what I was doing, they didn't ask.

"Did you at least call the cops?" I asked.

"Yeah," Bat's eyebrows drew together. "Although I didn't know what to tell them."

I pulled out my phone to make the call myself when the elevator dinged, and a uniformed officer stepped out and headed for the bar.

"Officer Demarzio," he said, holding up a badge. "I'm looking for Bat Keller. Something about a disturbance?"

Bat raised a hand. "That's me. I made the call, but you'll want to talk to her." He pointed in my direction and went back to pouring drinks like everything was normal.

"Good evening, officer." I set Courtney's drink on the bar. "You'll want to get that tested."

Demarzio glared at me. "What exactly do you think we'll find?"

"Did that guy put something in my drink?" Courtney asked. "Is that why you took it from me?"

"I'll ask the questions here," Demarzio said, trying to gain control.

"Never, ever, leave your drink unattended at the

bar," I told her, a slight scolding tone in my voice. "I'm pretty sure he tried to roofie you."

Courtney's eyes widened. "You mean..."

The officer cleared his throat. "How much of it did you drink?"

"None of it," she said. "Thanks to Whit. She's a hero. You should have seen her practically jump off—"

"I'm sure the officer is busy," I interrupted her. I didn't think he'd be nearly as impressed by my antics as Courtney and the others had been.

The officer pulled out a plastic container—sort of a cup with screw-on lid—and poured the remainder of the drink into it, then wrote on the label. "I'll send this to the lab, but it'll be several days minimum before they get to it. An attempted drugging is going to be lower priority."

"What about attempted murder?" I asked. "The guy pulled a gun on me."

Courtney gasped. "What?"

Officer Demarzio frowned, as if annoyed I'd created more work for him. "I'll need you to come to the station tomorrow and file a report."

Great. Just how I wanted to spend an afternoon.

As soon as the officer left, Bat pulled me aside to get the whole story. His expression changed as he considered what might have happened.

"Thanks, Whit," he said. "Courtney's right. You really are a hero."

"Aw, it was nothing," I said, basking in his praise and waiting for more accolades.

After several long moments of silence, he asked, "Can you cover the bar for the rest of the evening? I want to take my sister home."

"Sure." We closed in an hour anyway, so I figured I could handle it. "I've got you covered."

He seemed somewhat doubtful but nodded. "Try not to burn the place down, okay?"

I grinned. "Cover the bar. Don't burn it down. Got it. Anything else?"

He shook his head. "Maybe I should stay, just in case."

"Jenny's here." I waved him away. "She's got enough sense for both of us."

"Thank goodness for that."

A couple of people called out to me as they left, "That was awesome," or similar compliments. It's like they'd never seen someone jump off the side of a building before.

Chapter Five

While I waited for my shift to end, I lined up the rows of liquor bottles neatly and wiped down the bar until it shined.

Jenny turned off the last heat lamp then helped me close out the register. "It's way easier these days. Not so much money to count now that hardly anyone uses cash."

She retrieved her purse. "Ready?" When I nodded, she pressed the button for the elevator, and I came out from behind the bar.

"How long have you worked here?" I asked to break the silence while we waited.

"Ten years. I never would have stayed so long but the tips are good. The real reason I'm still here is that Bat is the best boss ever."

The elevator dinged as it opened, and we stepped

inside. We made small talk as it slowly descended, and I couldn't help thinking I'd be halfway home by now if I'd taken the stairs.

When we stepped onto the empty sidewalk and said goodnight, I headed for the beach, remembering the feel of the sand on my sore feet. The silver glow of the full moon lit my path, its beams dancing on the waves.

Slipping off my boots, I let my bare feet sink into the cool sand as the stress of the evening began to melt away. I pulled my jacket closer against the chilly ocean breeze as I hurried home. As I walked next to the path, preferring the sand to the hard cement, the rhythm of the crashing waves matched the ebb and flow of my swirling thoughts.

Everything that had happened that evening made sense until the creep pulled a gun on me. Even that didn't throw me like the arrival of the black sedan. I'd always assumed predators worked alone.

Lost in my own thoughts, I nearly walked past the cottage. I wiped most of the sand from my feet and unlocked the patio door. As tired as I was, I debated whether to take off my clothes or just climb into bed fully dressed.

I stumbled over something in the dark. Something that yelped.

I yelped too, then flipped on the light. A small

furry dog gazed up at me with big brown eyes as if wondering what I was doing there.

"I'll ask the questions here, Mister." I peeked at its underside and corrected myself. "I mean, Missy. Where the heck did you come from?" She couldn't be more than five or six pounds from the looks of her—maybe less under all that brown and white fur. She cocked her head first one way and then the other.

"I'm Whitley," I said to the dog. "But you can call me Whit. And you are?"

The dog didn't answer—no surprise there. After a search of the living room, she followed me to the kitchen where I found a bag of dog food along with a leash and a note. I recognized my mother's perfect cursive.

"Dear Whitley." I read the note out loud, mimicking her voice as well as I could. "I thought you would like to have a dog since you're there all alone. Feed it twice a day, and don't let it go pee-pee on the carpet. Love, Mother."

I crumpled the note into a ball and threw it hard against the wall. It barely made a thud, which wasn't satisfying at all, so I picked up the bag of dog food and threw that. It burst open.

Great. Now I'd have to clean it up.

The tiny dog ran from the room in apparent terror and barely managed to squeeze under the sofa in the living room. I wasn't going to let it make me feel guilty. I had enough trouble trying to take care of myself.

I called my mother, and was surprised when she picked up, considering the late hour.

"I don't like dogs," I said.

"Of course, you do, dear," she responded. "It's cats you don't like."

"I'm allergic to cats. I don't like dogs, but if I did like dogs, I'd want a big dog, like a Doberman Pincher or a Great Dane, not a, a—" I peered under the sofa for another look. "What is this runt of a dog, anyway?"

"It's a Chihuahua mix. I saw her picture online and knew you'd just love her. The rescue organization wanted to meet you first, but I assured them that you'd make an excellent dog owner. They were so nice, they delivered her right to our door."

"Right," I said, beginning to seethe. "You mean you wrote them a big check."

"They rely on donations. Otherwise, how could they save those poor creatures from being euthanized?"

I paced back and forth in the kitchen, trying to control my temper. She was not going to manipulate me into doing her bidding. Not this time. "I want you to come tomorrow and pick up the dog. I don't have time to take care of it."

"I can't do that," she said. "I'm driving up to the mountains to see your grandmother."

I had a brilliant thought. "Why don't you take the dog to her?"

"Don't be silly. I'm not going to drive two hours with a dog in the car. It will get lint all over the leather."

"Fur. Dogs shed fur, not lint." I was too tired to argue. "I'll call you tomorrow to arrange to take the dog back. Good night." I hung up before she could get in the last word.

Two bowls sat on the floor on a tea towel, no doubt to protect the mahogany parquet from water stains. After sweeping up the scattered kibble, I refilled the water bowl and searched for something the dog could sleep on. In the linen closet, I found a plush blanket that I folded and placed next to the food and water bowls.

"Goodnight, dog," I said. "Don't get too comfortable. This is only temporary."

When I emerged from the bathroom, the dog was waiting for me, wagging her tail expectantly. I ignored her and climbed into bed.

As I was drifting off to sleep, I heard a soft whine. Closing my eyes tightly, I ignored the sound, which only got louder. Rolling over, I saw the dog eyeing me from the floor. She lifted her furry ears like a begging child.

I was firm. "Don't even think about it."

She whined again.

I was unbending. "Go to sleep."

She whimpered.

My body ached for sleep. I grabbed her by her harness and plopped her on top of the comforter. She burrowed underneath the covers, and soon we were both asleep.

Chapter Six

I woke from a wonderful dream that might have featured a certain bartender, only to realize the tongue licking my face belonged to a five-pound dog.

"Ugh." I pushed her away, but she must have thought I wanted to play, because she began tugging at my tee shirt and making yipping sounds. "Okay, okay. I'm getting up."

After making a pot of coffee and refilling the runt's food dish, I pulled out my phone. When my mother didn't answer my call, I sent her a text message, then about a dozen more. The evil queen didn't respond to a single one. I started calling rescue organizations to find out where the dog had come from, so I could give her back.

I reached people at three of the rescue organizations, but they disavowed knowledge of the dog. The other calls went to voicemail, so I left messages.

She'd be a great dog for someone else. Not me. Stunt work required long hours on the set, sometimes seven days a week when we were shooting. She'd be much happier in a suburban home in the valley with 2.5 kids. Not too young, mind you, because they might drop her or step on her. Not that I cared. I didn't.

"I suppose you need to go for a walk." I grabbed the leash, and the little mutt jumped a foot or two off the floor repeatedly. "Your tricks do not impress me," I assured her. I was a runner, not a walker, and there was no way she'd be able to keep up with me.

I poured myself a cup of coffee and she followed me to the patio door, squeezing outside the moment I opened it. She sniffed every corner of the patio, watering one of the shrubs, then looked at me expectantly.

A waist-high wall separated the patio from the walking, running, and bike path, and beyond that was sand and sea. Attaching the leash, I leaned over and plopped her onto the other side of the wall onto a narrow strip of grass so she could do her business. She barked at a few people and tried to chase a bike, so I hoisted her back over the wall and we went inside.

After a run along the beach, a shower, and a second cup of coffee, I hadn't solved either question bothering me. The first had to do with the lowlife I'd chased the night before. Was he working for someone? Part of a scumbag gang? That seemed unlikely.

The second question—what to do about the dog—would have to wait until my mother responded. By lunchtime, I began to think she was purposely ignoring me.

My stomach grumbled, and I made myself a sandwich under the watchful eye of my temporary canine roommate.

"No people food for you." If I started feeding her from my plate, she'd bug me at every meal. When she sat up on her haunches and fluttered her big brown eyes at me, I lost my resolve. A little bite of turkey wouldn't hurt.

By the time I headed off to the hotel for my shift, I still bristled at my over-controlling mother. The warm sand under my feet and rhythmic waves did nothing to distract me from my annoyance.

Bat greeted me as I stepped behind the bar. "You okay?"

"Sure, except my mom got me a dog. Who gets someone a dog without asking them?"

"How dare she."

"Right?" I said, before seeing the look on his face. "Oh, sarcasm." I had a thought. "Do you like dogs? She's super cute and would be a great chick magnet. Oh, but you already have a chick, I mean fiancée. I bet what's-her-name would like a little dog. She could carry it around in her purse."

"I don't think so," he said.

"Yeah, you're probably right." I agreed. "Deborah looks more like a Shih Tzu type of woman. No worries. I'm sure someone will want her. She doesn't eat much, and she's mostly potty trained."

Bat raised his eyebrows. "Mostly?"

"It's not important." I grabbed a few lemons and started slicing them vigorously.

"Whoa." Bat took the knife from me. "Why don't you restock the cherries and olives."

The bar began to fill as the sun headed for the horizon. Courtney came upstairs on her break, and Bat motioned to one of the tables too far away for me to eavesdrop. She didn't seem like her usual bouncy, sunshiny self. They talked for nearly half an hour, and when she finally stood, she glanced in my direction giving me a weak smile before returning to the lobby.

"What's with your sister? I know she almost got roofied last night, but it could have been worse." Much worse in fact, but I didn't want to think about that.

"Yeah." He seemed distracted.

"Earth to Bat," I said.

"That's original."

"Hey, it's not easy writing all your own material. Those guys on TV make it look easy, but they've got a team of writers. Is something else going on?"

"I'm selling the hotel," he said.

"Really? But just the other day, you said—"

"Hey." A guy at the end of the bar waved like he was dying of thirst. "Can I get a drink over here?"

"Keep your shirt on," I called back. "Can't you see we're busy?"

Bat gave me one of his long-suffering looks and went to take the guy's order.

"You don't have to sell the hotel just to get rid of me," I said. "There are easier ways."

The customer looked concerned. "You're selling the hotel?"

"Big mouth," Bat said to me. "Would you see what Jenny needs, please?"

Jenny tapped her nails on the side of her tray as she waited at the service bar.

"Fine," I said to Bat. "We'll talk later."

While I filled Jenny's order, I whispered, "Do you know why Bat suddenly decided to sell the hotel? Just the other day it sounded like that was the last thing on his mind."

She shook her head. "What am I supposed to do if he sells this place?"

I shrugged. "Get another job?" Server jobs seemed like they'd be plentiful in this town.

"It's not that easy." She took the gin and tonics I handed her, slipping a lime wedge onto the edge of each glass. "I have to work around my kids schedule, and a lot of bar owners aren't as understanding as Bat."

"You've got kids?" How did I not know she was a mom?

"Two boys." Her tense expression softened, replaced by a smile. "Six and eight. They're the cutest rascals you've ever seen. I'll show you pictures later."

Soon the bar filled up with happy-hour customers, and I was too busy serving half-priced drinks and appetizers to give me time to think about anything else. Just as the crowd began to thin, Bat slipped away.

Courtney emerged from the elevator and sat at the end of the bar, throwing her purse on the chair next to her. I didn't blame her for wanting to keep her distance from the other bar patrons. People just love to ask nosy questions.

"So, are you doing okay?" My question didn't count.

"I don't really want to talk about it." She looked past me.

I looked over my shoulder, following her gaze. When had Bat returned? Watching him casually lean over the bar made my mind wander, and then I remembered I was attempting to have a conversation. I leaned forward and whispered, "You mean about selling the hotel?"

"No, I mean about global warming," she snipped. "Of course, I mean selling the hotel."

"Oh, good one," I said appreciatively. "I think I'm starting to have an influence on you."

"Great," came Bat's voice from behind me. "Just what I need. One sarcastic coworker is more than enough for me."

"There's nothing wrong with standing up for yourself." I turned my back on him and returned my attention to Courtney. "Want me to make you a drink?"

"No, definitely not. I may never drink again."

"You only say that because you've never had my special signature drink." That got raised eyebrows from her and a laugh from Bat.

"Let me guess," he said. "It's dark and bitter."

"Just the way I like my men." I winked at Courtney and turned back to Bat. "You can leave now."

He straightened up to his full six foot two. "This is my bar."

"Go over there." I motioned to the other end of the bar. After a moment of hesitation, he complied.

With not much idea about what I was doing, I picked up a shaker and began to pour in anything that sounded yummy, starting with chocolate liqueur and Bailey's. I added a shot of Cointreau for a touch of orange flavor, shook it until I was sure it was good and chilled, and poured it into a martini glass. It had a nice foam on top, but it needed more.

Courtney watched me take a Twix bar out of my purse, chop it up, and sprinkle it on top.

Hoping it tasted as good as it looked, I presented it to Courtney with a flourish. She gave it a suspicious look then took a taste.

"Yum." She had the biggest smile I'd seen her wear since the guy tried to drug her. She took another sip and put the glass down. "I still don't want to talk about it."

"I don't want to talk about global warming either," I said. "What do you want to talk about?"

She considered my question before answering. "Let's talk about you."

"My favorite subject," I said. "I can tell you all about how amazing I am. Did you know I did all the stunts for Emma Turner in the last *Avengers* movie?"

"That's cool." She gave me a doting smile. "How did you get to be a stuntwoman?"

"I was a gymnast. Almost went to the Olympics."

"Really?"

People always loved hearing this story. "As an alternate. My mother was so disappointed that I missed making the team." When I saw the look of pity she gave me, I remembered why I hated telling it.

"But alternates get to go to the Olympics. Why do you say you almost went?"

"It's a long story," I said, asking myself why I went down this particular fork on memory lane.

"I have time," she said.

I thought about telling her about how my mother chastised me for putting on weight, telling me that's why I was "just" an alternate, and how I proceeded to starve myself and ended up in the hospital. I thought about it for maybe a second. "You know how you don't want to talk about global warming?"

"Oh," she said, taking another sip of her drink. "You don't want to talk about the Olympics?"

I bit my tongue to keep myself from sharing one of my fun, sarcastic comments. "Anyway, when I moved on from gymnastics, I discovered Parkour, and that was the best thing that ever happened to me."

"Parkour?" The blank look on her face told me she'd never heard of it.

"Parkour came out of military obstacle training, but it's evolved since then. It's basically getting from one place to another while climbing, jumping, crawling—pretty much whatever is the most efficient. What I do these days is called free running, since I like to incorporate flips and tricks to keep it fun. I get bored easily." I pulled out my phone and showed her a video filmed the previous year in downtown Los Angeles of me running and jumping over concrete ledges and metal railings.

"Wow. Aren't you afraid of getting injured? If you landed wrong on one of those railings, I bet it would hurt."

"It does, trust me. And when I'm working on a film, I'm forbidden from doing it. The minute I finish a shoot, I'm off and running again. Nothing makes me feel more alive."

"Can I come watch you do it sometime?" Courtney looked at me hopefully, like I was her new best friend. "I can film you if you want."

"I like to go it alone." I didn't want a new best friend. Besides, I wouldn't know what to do with one if I had one. "I only had it filmed that time because I was up for a commercial and they wanted to see me in action."

It wasn't the first time I'd disappointed Courtney. If she were smart, she'd start hanging out with people she had something in common with. They could share makeup tips and talk about boys.

For the next hour, she watched me serve drinks and wash glasses in silence. The next time I made it to her end of the bar, her mood had turned somber again.

"Want another one?" I said, not sure if I could recreate it.

She shook her head. "I don't know why he's doing it," she said quietly and without emotion, as if she was telling me the weather.

"Doing what?"

"Selling the hotel. They said one way or another he'd end up selling it to them. He said, 'over my dead body.'" She took the last sip of her drink and stood. "Then they said, 'Maybe not *your* dead body.'"

"Who is *they*?" I asked, but she seemed a million miles away. "Or 'who *are* they' is proper grammar I suppose."

Instead of answering me, she said, "I'll see you."

I watched her walk toward the elevator. Someone wanted to buy the hotel and they would do anything to get it, including making death threats. Not cool.

"It's not your problem, Whit," I told myself, but I had an issue with bullies going back to third grade when Johnny Peterson tried to take my best friend's lunch money. Sure, I got sent to the principal's office and was grounded for a month, but it was worth it.

No one was going to take advantage of Bat and Courtney. Not while I was around.

Trying to make sense of the past two day's events had given me a headache. At the end of my shift, I walked home looking forward to a hot bath and a cold drink, maybe not in that order. The moment I stepped through the patio door, I caught a whiff of Chanel Number 5. The bath would have to wait.

Chapter Seven

I sucked in my breath, ready to hold it until I turned blue, when I recognized a different smell. The warm, earthy scent of Patchouli.

I ran into the living room. A woman in layers of organic cotton with wavy, gray hair past her shoulders grinned the moment she saw me.

"Whitley!" My grandmother stood, dropping the dog from her lap onto the floor. "Sorry, little fella," she said to the Chihuahua. "I forgot you were there."

"It's a girl," I said. "What are you doing here, Bobbie?"

"Ask your mother. She thinks I'm too old and frail to handle a little ice and snow." She held her arms out wide for a hug, and I took care not to squeeze her tiny frame too hard. Before I could slip away, she pinched my cheek.

"Ouch." I rubbed my face. Maybe she wasn't as frail as she looked. "Is my mother still here?"

Right on cue, Angela entered from the kitchen, wearing impeccably tailored slacks and her favorite Gucci slingbacks. To complete the ensemble, she carried a goblet of white wine. "Where were you at this time of night?"

"Nice to see you too," I said. "You should have told me you were coming. I would have done the dishes."

"You didn't tell her?" Bobbie shook her head and gave me a sympathetic look, probably glad she and her daughter-in-law weren't related by blood. But then neither was I.

My origin story was long and convoluted, one that I avoided having to explain. Bobbie 's daughter, a free spirit living in South America, got pregnant and gave up the baby, aka me. Bobbie's son, my biological uncle, and his wife Angela adopted me, and we all lived happily ever after. Sort of.

Forcing myself back to the present, I asked, "Why didn't you call me? Or text?"

"I had enough trouble convincing Roberta to come stay here. I wasn't in the mood to have a debate with you as well." Angela settled into the sofa, crossed her long legs, and took a slow sip of her wine.

Bobbie rolled her eyes and stage-whispered to me, "How do I get her to stop calling me that?"

"It is your name," Angela huffed.

"She's got you there." I considered suggesting that we could go to the courthouse and get it changed legally, but I figured I'd wait until my mother left before mentioning it.

Pretty much everyone except my mother thought the name Bobbie fit my hippy-dippy grandmother much better than Roberta. She was healthy, financially self-sufficient, and capable of making her own decisions, and yet my mother fussed over her, telling her what to do. My mother claimed to worry about Bobbie, but I think it was a control issue.

"I'm going home," Angela said. "Call me if you need anything."

"Wait." I chased her to the door. "Take the dog with you."

"Don't be ridiculous. Do you think I'm going to risk getting dog hair on these slacks?"

"Then tell me the name of the rescue so I can give her back," I demanded.

She gave me one of her imperious gazes. "Stop it, right now. The dog is yours, and that's final."

"No." I said. I was tired of her acting like she could tell me what to do, the way she did everyone else, even her mother-in-law, Bobbie.

"If you want to stay here, rent free I might add, then you will do as you're told."

Standing by the front door, watching her walk to the car, I felt both like a scolded toddler and a rebellious teenager. The one thing my mother never made me feel like was a grown woman. I resisted the urge to slam the door and returned to the living room where the dog and my grandmother had made themselves comfortable.

"I guess you're stuck with both of us," Bobbie said.

"Let me help you get settled in." I looked around for a suitcase. "Where are your things?"

"I'm all settled, my little Miss Whit. We arrived hours ago."

I smiled at her old nickname for me. "Well, it's late, so I'll let you get some sleep."

"Do I look like some old lady who needs her beauty rest?" Bobbie paused a moment for effect, and added, "Don't answer that." She patted the sofa next to her. "Sit down and tell me what you've been up to since I've seen you."

We polished off the very expensive wine that my mother had opened, and I told Bobbie about my new job, my new boss, and his sister.

Then I told her about the guy who drugged Court-ney's drink. Bobbie loved a mystery, especially true crime, and she wanted all the details.

"Oh, that reminds me." I pulled the cherry jar with the drink sample out of my bag. "Do you know where we could get this tested for drugs?" I figured it couldn't hurt to ask her. My grandmother was surpris-ingly resourceful.

She thought for a moment. "Like a lab?"

"I suppose so."

"Not off the top of my head."

Maybe the police would share their findings, but I'd heard that results could take days or longer. I was almost positive Courtney's drink had been dosed with Rohypnol, commonly known as roofies or the forget-me drug, but I wanted to know for sure.

"What about running license plates?" I asked.

"I might be able to help with that," Bobbie said. "My friend Darla's grandson works at the DMV. She's a bit embarrassed about it, and who can blame her. Ugh. Government work." She shuddered. "I'll call her and see if he'll run them."

"Great." I was extremely curious to know who owned the car that picked up the lowlife who tried to drug Courtney.

"Tell me more about your new job," Bobbie said. "Since when do you tend bar?"

At least she didn't shudder again. "It's just something to do until I get another gig with the studios. I've only been working a few days, but they seem like good people."

"I'll have to meet them so I can judge for myself," Bobbie said as she poured the last of the wine into her glass. "I'm an excellent judge of character."

"You're an excellent judge of charac*ters*. The wacky kind. That's a completely different thing."

My grandmother had married a wealthy and eccentric man. My grandfather had made millions from his inventions and started Leland Industries before he passed away a few years ago. Their son, my adopted dad, didn't have a wacky bone in his body, but he had a head for business and grew the family company into an international conglomerate.

Bobbie and I loved to talk about all the crazy relatives, much to the horror of my parents, who preferred to pretend they didn't exist. There was Great Aunt Ophelia, who became a Buddhist nun, and her brother Jerome, who claimed he could talk to the dead.

My parents always seemed reluctant when they sent me to spend the summer with my grandmother, probably concerned she'd be a bad influence on me. She was the sort of grandmother who put extra marshmallows in your cocoa after you ate the first batch off the top and let you watch R-rated movies if you promised not to tell your parents.

Bobbie interrupted my walk down memory lane. "Why don't you open another bottle of wine?"

"Okay, but if anybody asks, it was your idea. And by 'anyone,' I mean Angela."

We chatted until four in the morning when I waved the metaphorical white flag and stumbled off to bed. The dog followed Bobbie to her room, the ungrateful little runt.

Chapter Eight

A loud ringing woke me way too early the next morning. As I rolled over and grabbed the phone, a yelp nearly made me drop it. The Chihuahua wiggled out from under the covers and gave my chin a lick.

"Yuck." I wiped off the slobber with my sleeve. "I thought you were in Bobbie's room, you little sneak." I held her back with one hand while I looked at the display. My mother. Letting the call go to voicemail, I climbed out of bed and threw on my running clothes.

I smelled coffee. There were perks to having your grandmother stay with you. "I'm going for a run," I called out as I slipped through the patio door. "Be back in thirty."

My shift didn't start until four, so after I got back from my run and showered, I had hours to kill. Bobbie and I sipped coffee on the patio while I made fun of the tourists walking by. Turned out that also meant listening to the dog bark at every passing person.

Within minutes, Bobbie had the dog behaving like a model citizen and eating out of her hand. Literally, which is probably why the dog stopped barking.

A Japanese couple and their daughter walked by, and the dog ran to the edge of the patio wagging her tail. The little girl laughed and pointed. "Kitsune, kitsune."

"It means fox," the father explained. "She thinks your dog looks like a fox."

I gave the Chihuahua a closer look. She was the spitting image of a fox, if only she had a fluffier tail.

"Kitsune, kitsune," the girl repeated, and I picked up the dog so she could pet her. I considered asking them if they wanted to take the dog with them, but when I looked back at Bobbie, she shook her head. How did she know what I was thinking?

After the father coaxed the child away, Bobbie said, "Sounds like the perfect name for her."

"What are you talking about?"

"Kitsune," she said. "The dog needs a name, after all."

I sighed, feeling helpless in the face of the inevitable. "If we give her a name, we'll never get rid of her."

"Is that so terrible?"

"Kit for short?" I suggested.

"Perfect," she agreed. Then she chuckled. "Whit and Kit, my two wayward granddaughters."

❦ ❧

When I arrived at the lounge for my shift, a few mid-afternoon diners lingered enjoying the ocean view, but the bar was empty. I whipped up a fresh batch of sour mix while Bat noisily moved bottles around, checking to see what to get from the storeroom. I'd almost forgotten that Bobbie wanted to meet my boss and his sister until I heard my name along with the sound of huffing and puffing.

"Hi, Bobbie," I said. "We have an elevator."

"You don't stay in shape," she paused for a breath, "by taking the elevator."

I raised my eyebrows. Staying in shape had never been the goal of anyone in my family except for me. Thin, yes. In shape? Not so much.

"You also don't have a heart attack taking the elevator." I didn't usually dole out health advice, but this was more common sense. And I loved sharing my commonsense suggestions, even if no one else appreciated them.

Bobbie pulled up a barstool and quickly became distracted, and I knew why. She motioned me over. "Is that your boss?"

One look at her face and I knew Bat had another conquest whether he wanted it or not. "I think you have a little drool, right there," I pointed to a corner of her mouth.

"Very funny," she said. "Aren't you going to introduce me?"

I called Bat over and made the introductions.

"Very nice to meet you, Bobbie," Bat said, taking her hand and giving her the warmest of smiles. "Why don't I make you something special to drink."

"I can do that," I offered.

"That's all right, Whit," Bobbie said. "I can have you make me a drink anytime. Let me see what Bat has to offer."

Did she really say that? "Okay. I'll just be over here washing glasses if you need me."

I listened to them chat while I worked. Bat made Bobbie laugh, and then Bobbie made Bat laugh. A few regulars sidled up to the bar, and I served them while keeping one ear on Bobbie and my boss's conversation.

Bat finally tore himself away from my grandmother as the bar filled up. As soon as I had a free moment, I made my way back over to her. I kept my voice low, hoping not to be overheard. Luckily, no one seemed interested in our conversation.

"So, what do you think?" I asked.

"He's charming," Bobbie said. "Simply charming."

"That's what they said about Ted Bundy, if I recall correctly."

"And he's so handsome," she said. "Is he single?"

"Engaged." I saw the look on her face. "Don't look so disappointed. Maybe his grandfather is single, and I can hook you up."

She pursed her lips. "I can get my own dates, thank you very much."

I didn't even want to know what she meant by that. "Was Courtney in the lobby when you got here?"

"Yes. A lovely girl. We had a nice, long conversation."

"About the guy who tried to drug her drink?" I knew Bobbie was curious about what had happened to Courtney, and she wasn't afraid to ask sensitive or embarrassing questions.

Bobbie seemed appalled. "That's not how one starts a conversation, dear. I told her I was your grandmother. She, of course, couldn't believe anyone who looked as young as me could possibly have a granddaughter your age."

"So, did you go over your cosmetic procedures with her?"

Bobbie shot me a withering glare. "That would be your mother. I told her about my skin care regimen and gave her a few pointers."

I smiled at her rationalization. No doubt, the lotions and elixirs she used didn't hurt, but she wasn't above getting a Botox injection now and then. I decided to drop the subject. After all, the last time my mother suggested that I go to her dermatologist to take care of my worry lines, I actually considered it for a moment.

"This drink is delightful," Bobbie said, loudly enough for Bat to hear.

I glanced over my shoulder and saw Bat heading our way.

"Glad you enjoyed it." Bat gave her another charming smile, and added, "On the house, of course."

"Oh, you don't have to do that," Bobbie said, but she didn't reach for her wallet. She turned back to me. "I'll see you at home later." Lowering her voice, she added, "If Courtney's still at her post, I'll ask her about the drugging. Maybe I can coax her into revealing a clue she's overlooked."

"A clue?" I asked. Bobbie loved a good mystery, but this was real life. "Just try not to upset her, okay? She seems pretty shaken up by everything." This time I lowered my voice, not wanting Bat to overhear me. "But see if she'll tell you anything about why Bat's decided to sell the hotel."

She nodded and I watched, relieved to see her push the button for the elevator.

The next couple of hours flew by as the happy hour crowd was replaced by the dinner crowd. Bat sent me home shortly after eight when the crowd began to thin. At his suggestion, I ordered an appetizer plate to take home to share with Bobbie. I asked the chef if he had a bone, but that earned me a lecture about not giving bones to dogs. Next came a request for pictures of my new dog.

"What do you mean you don't have pictures of your dog?" His shock equaled his disappointment.

"I'll take some tonight and show you on my next shift," I promised, grabbing my bag and escaping before I got another lecture.

At the cottage, Bobbie poured us each a glass of wine while I divvied up the bruschetta and calamari. Kit followed us out to the patio, hoping we'd drop a morsel. She sat on her haunches with her front paws in the air until Bobbie tossed her a chunk of squid.

I leaned back in my chaise lounge and gazed across the sand at the breaking waves. "We're so lucky to be here at the beach on a warm fall evening. Here it is October, and we can still sit outside enjoying the ocean breeze and the—"

"And the smell of the rotting seaweed?" Bobbie interrupted. "I wish I were home in Arrow Springs. In the mountains, at this time of year, there's a nip in the air, and the scent of pine. The needles make a crunch, crunch, crunch sound when you walk around the neighborhood. I miss that sound."

"And the ice goes crunch, crunch, crunch, just before you fall and break a hip."

"My bones are in excellent condition," she huffed. "The doctors have told me I'm at no more risk of breaking a hip than someone half my age."

"Have you told my parents that?" As soon as I said it, I knew it was a stupid question.

"Since when does your mother listen? And my son kowtows to her no matter what she says. He tells me Angela only wants what's best for me. Ha! She probably brought me here so I would keep an eye on you."

I sighed.

"Oh, I'm sorry." She sounded contrite. "This is your mother I'm talking about. Sometimes I forget."

"That's okay. It's not like we share DNA."

Bobbie sat up straight. "Don't say that. You know Angela loves you."

"Yeah, yeah, she just has a hard time showing it. Just because you keep saying it, doesn't make it true." Angela was not a hugs-and-cookies kind of mom. And, she was a control freak, which was probably why Bobbie and I frustrated her. She couldn't control either of us.

"Will you ever cut her a break?" Bobbie asked. "It's not her fault your real mother gave you up. Someday, you need to forgive both of them."

I ignored her comment. "Maybe I'm supposed to be watching you. Or she figured she'd kill two birds with one stone and have us watch each other."

"Kind of like having the Kitsune watch the hen house, don't you think?"

At the sound of her name, Kit came running over and jumped in Bobbie's lap. She nuzzled Bobbie's hand, no doubt asking for ear scratches or hoping for leftovers.

"She knows her name already? It's only been a day."

"We've been practicing." Bobbie scratched the dog's ears. "Haven't we, Kitsune, huh?" Kit wagged her tail and licked her ear. "Who's a good girl?"

"I thought we agreed on Kit," I said. "I have enough trouble getting people to call me Whitley instead of Whitney. I can only imagine what they'll do with Kitsune. I wish they would have named me Ann or Beth or something easy."

"No, you don't." Bobbie started baby talking to Kit again. "No, she doesn't, does she? She loves her name. She was named after the town in England where I met her grandfather."

"I already know this story," I said. What was it with old people telling you the same story over and over?

"Yes, but Kit hasn't heard it."

Kit tilted her head at the sound of her name. She did a few circles on Bobbie's lap then curled up with her fluffy tail wrapped around her and closed her eyes.

"She's not interested in the story either."

Bobbie held out her wine glass. "Would you pour me another?"

"Won't Mom be mad if we drink all her best wine?"

"She's got cases of the stuff, so I doubt she'll even notice." She wiggled her glass. "Hurry up. My arm's getting tired."

"She'll notice," I said, but headed to the kitchen to retrieve the bottle. When I returned, I refilled her glass. "What should we do tomorrow? I've got the day off."

"Oh, good. I think we should visit the police station and see if they've had the drink tested."

I almost spilled the wine. That was exactly what I'd planned to do, but not with my grandmother tagging along. "You've been watching too much Law and Order. I doubt if they'll have results yet."

"If they haven't, then we'll find a lab and get your sample tested ourselves. You'd be surprised how money can speed things up."

"Okay, I suppose." A field trip to the police station would be a change of pace, and even if they wouldn't tell us anything, I might get some details to put in my screenplay. I hadn't touched it in months, so it was about time to revisit it.

Bobbie took the last bite of bruschetta and set her plate on the table. "I'll call Darla again and see if she got us the information on the owner of the black sedan."

I could almost see the wheels turning in her head as she planned her next move. She was having way too much fun with something she probably shouldn't be getting involved in.

"Once we have an address," she continued, "we can stop by and ask the owner of the car some questions."

"Hold on," I said. "Do you think that's safe?"

"Safe? I've spent my whole life being safe. I think it's about time I was more reckless." Lying in her chair with a sleeping dog on her lap, she looked the opposite of reckless. "But I'll do it on my own if you're concerned."

"I am concerned. About you." I'd never known my grandmother to do anything that even hinted of abandon. To my knowledge, she'd never skydived, bungee-jumped or had an affair. She probably never even flirted with another man while my grandfather was alive. "If you get hurt or killed on my watch, my parents will never let me hear the end of it."

She smiled as though she knew she had me in a double bind. "Then you'll have to come along to make sure I don't get into any trouble."

I sighed. If my mother thought we would keep an eye on each other, she wouldn't be happy when she heard about the two of us investigating a crime.

Chapter Nine

The best time to go for my run was first thing in the morning before I woke up enough to talk myself out of it. If I even waited for the coffee to brew, my chances of getting any exercise dropped by at least fifty percent.

After a quick warmup on the patio, I took off heading north, the beach to my left and buildings to the right. Cottages gave way to hotels and restaurants as I approached the main part of town. Just past Hotel Elegance stood the more modest Sandpiper Inn. Both had been built on a small cliff, maybe ten or fifteen feet high.

As I slowed to a walk, it occurred to me that the two lots would be the perfect size for a new, more upscale hotel or perhaps condominiums. Whoever was trying to buy Hotel Elegance might have had the same idea. That seemed like something worth looking into.

Narrow wooden steps led up the side of the cliff to the back of the Sandcastle and a small veranda. Following the path, I found the hotel's rear entrance and stepped inside. A long hallway led to a small lobby where I found a round-faced, middle-aged man behind the reception desk.

Pasting a friendly smile on my face, I called out, "Good morning." My shoes squeaked on the tile floors.

He returned my greeting warmly, adding, "May I be of assistance?"

"Maybe. I was just passing by, and I got curious. Who's the owner of the Sandcastle?"

A scowl flashed for a split second before his customer service smile returned. "We've just been sold. We were owned by the same family for nearly forty years. I've worked here for twenty years myself, but I guess all good things must come to an end."

"Sorry to hear that," I said sincerely. "This town is not going to be the same without the Sandpiper and Hotel Elegance."

He shook his head sadly. "So many of the older buildings are being torn down in the name of progress. I just don't get it."

"So, it is being torn down then?" I asked.

He seemed to have realized he'd said too much.

"Nothing concrete from what I understand. I really shouldn't be repeating rumors."

The clerk didn't have much more information to share with me, or perhaps he'd decided it would be best not to say more.

As I headed back to the cottage, I couldn't get it out of my head that the town where I spent summers as a young child would be gone soon, or at least it would look very different.

During the run back, I repeated the man's words to myself. "All good things must come to an end." Was that true?

When I entered the cottage, I found Bobbie humming in the kitchen.

"What are you so cheerful about this morning?" I grumbled. Mornings did not bring out the best in me, and the idea of buildings being torn down in the name of progress didn't help.

"Go on out to the patio and I'll bring you your coffee." She continued humming as I walked past her.

"Thanks. Give me a few." As tempting as coffee sounded, it would have to wait. "Shower first. Then coffee."

Feeling like a new woman, I found Bobbie on the patio with two mugs of coffee and Kit on her lap. I pulled the Afghan off the chaise lounge and wrapped it around me before joining her at the glass patio table. A few pedestrians and bicyclists passed by, but traffic on the path was always light this time of year. Occasionally, a jogger would slow down and eye me enviously.

"Here you go." Bobbie pushed a plate of cookies across the table.

"Cookies for breakfast?" I asked. She obviously wanted something from me, and that made me apprehensive.

"They're oatmeal cookies," she said. "I don't know why people seem to think it's okay to have oatmeal full of brown sugar and who knows what else for breakfast, but for some reason, eating oatmeal cookies before noon is a no-no."

Okay, so she was a bit touchy this morning. "I wasn't complaining." I reached for a cookie. It was still warm. I took a bite and chewed slowly before washing it down with Ethiopian blend coffee.

Bobbie nudged Kit off her lap then stood. "Are you planning to spend all morning on the patio? I'd really like to get to the police station and get some answers."

I could take a hint. I grabbed another cookie and guzzled the last of my coffee. "Ready when you are."

During the short drive to the police station, Bobbie and I strategized. While I'd been on my run, she'd called ahead for the name of the detective in charge of the investigation.

"You can give them the sweet-little-old-lady

routine," I suggested. "By the way, how long have you been working that angle?"

"I'm not an old lady, and I don't know what you're talking about. You're a beautiful, young woman. Why don't you work that angle, as you say?" She paused to glance at me, adding, "Although, if that was your plan, you might have dressed more like a woman and less like a tomboy. Or a cat burglar."

"What's wrong with my outfit?" To call it an outfit was overselling it, but a black t-shirt, black jeans, and boots was my signature look. Not original, but it worked for me. And if I did need to break into some-place in the middle of the night, all I needed was a ski mask. Not that I was planning anything like that, but you never know.

"I say we try the direct approach," Bobbie suggested. "Just ask him straight out what drugs were found in the drink."

"And why are we asking?" I just thought I should be prepared in case they eager to share information.

"We're the public. We have a right to know."

"I see." We were almost at the station, so no time to come up with a better plan.

The police station sat next to the fire department, and they were both pleasantly designed in the Craftsman style that had become so popular shortly after most of the original Craftsman homes had been flattened. The inside had all the appeal one might expect from liberal use of Formica and beige paint.

Bobbie rang the bell on the counter three times. She rang it another three times. Then she began ringing it continuously.

"Don't you think they got the point?" I asked, but that didn't stop her.

"Apparently not, or someone would be here assisting us."

A woman in an official looking polo shirt came running over and grabbed the bell out of Bobbie's hand. "May I help you?" she asked, out of breath.

"There you are," Bobbie said. "We'd like to speak to Detective MacKenzie."

"And who should I tell him is asking for him?"

Bobbie leaned forward to read the woman's name tag. "Ellen, I'm Roberta Leland, and this is my grand-daughter, Whitley."

"Elena," she corrected her.

"No, my name is Roberta, but you can call me Bobbie. Everyone does. Except my daughter-in-law, but that's her mother, so I won't say any more than that."

"My name is Elena, not Ellen."

"Oh," Bobbie said. "Why didn't you say so?"

The woman gave her head a small shake as if to dislodge the crazy. I recognized the gesture. She left us at the front counter, taking the bell with her.

A tall, rather large man in an off-the-rack, polyester-blend suit emerged from a back room and approached the counter. One of the advantages of being raised by snooty parents is I can recognize polyester from a hundred yards.

"I'm Detective MacKenzie." His voice was professional with just a hint of warmth. "How can I help you ladies?"

"We're looking for some information," Bobbie said. "About the drugging at the Hotel Elegance."

"I see." His expression remained neutral as he glanced at me and back at Bobbie. "What kind of information?"

"My granddaughter Whitley," she gestured to me, "saw the perpetrator put something in one of her coworker's drinks. We were wondering if you could tell us what it was. I'm guessing it was a roofie."

The detective nodded as if he were about to tell us what we wanted to know, but instead he said, "I'm not able to discuss an ongoing investigation."

Bobbie turned to me. "You were right. The police aren't very cooperative at all. Good thing you got that sample." She turned back to the detective. "I don't suppose you know any local labs where we could get our own test done."

The detective opened his mouth to speak, but no sound came out for several seconds. Finally, he managed to say, "What do you mean, you have a sample?"

"My granddaughter is very resourceful."

"Any sample you have would not be able to be used as evidence in court," he said, his voice now stern.

Bobbie paused as if considering what he'd said. "Maybe not, but it will tell us what we want to know, which is what that man put in Courtney's drink. And if you won't tell us, then we'll have to use our own resources."

I decided to interrupt their staring contest. "Look," I said, tired of being on the sidelines. "I'm the one who called the cops that night. If you've read the report, you'll know I chased him for several blocks, and he pulled a gun on me before jumping into a black sedan." I left out the part about jumping off the side of the building. This wasn't the time to brag.

"Oh," he said. "That was you?"

"That reminds me," Bobbie said. "Have you had a chance to run the plates yet?"

The detective looked from me to Bobbie and back again. "I can't tell you who owns the car. Privacy regulations and all that. But I'll tell you what was in the drink if you promise not to get involved."

Bobbie and I nodded, but I was pretty sure she had her fingers crossed behind her back.

His gaze moved to me and back to Bobbie. "It was strychnine."

"Strychnine?" Bobbie and I said at the same time.

"But that's poison," I said. "I thought the guy drugged her so he could assault her. Why would he want to kill Courtney?"

"There wasn't a high enough dose to kill her. If she'd drunk it, she would have become ill, but it's unlikely she would have died. I can assure you, we are taking the matter very seriously and will investigate to our fullest capability. Now, if that's all—"

"It most certainly isn't," Bobbie said.

"Thank you, detective." I reached for her arm. "Let's go."

Bobbie shook me off and pointed a finger at him. "You better be investigating to your fullest capability, or I'll speak to the mayor," she said in a voice as threatening as she could muster. Which, to be honest, wouldn't terrify Kit.

Chasing after her as she stomped off, I stopped to glance back at the detective. His expression told me he was glad she was my problem and not his.

As she hurried across the parking lot, Bobbie asked, "Why would someone poison sweet, adorable Courtney?"

"No idea." My mind struggled with the same question.

"And why wasn't there enough poison to kill her?"

"That's a really good question. Maybe he failed

chemistry and didn't get the formula right." I unlocked the car and climbed in.

Bobbie got in on the passenger side, arranging the layers of organic fiber fabrics she called an outfit before buckling her seat belt. "I don't think the man you chased down was the mastermind of this attempted poisoning, do you?"

"Whoever planned it, wasn't much of a mastermind if he couldn't even measure the right dose." Something didn't make sense. A lot of things didn't make sense, come to think of it. "We need to find out who belongs to that license plate."

Bobbie shook her head. "Darla said she'd get back to me this afternoon. When we get home, I'll check my phone."

"You know, the new-fangled phones can go wherever you go."

"I don't want them knowing my every move. It's unsettling."

I considered asking her why she thought they, whoever "they" were, would be interested in her comings and goings, but I didn't want to go down that tin-foil-lined rabbit hole at that moment.

Instead, I suggested lunch.

"Let's go to the Cliffside Restaurant," Bobbie suggested, and gave me directions as if I were new to town.

Five minutes later, we were being led to a table on

the patio overlooking the ocean. Umbrellas protected us from the direct sun while a cool breeze kept the temperature at right about seventy-two degrees. A seagull perched on the railing squawked when I shooed him away.

The two best things about going to lunch with my grandmother were first, she had very expensive taste, and second, she always paid.

The worst thing was ordering.

"I'll have the butternut squash soup to start, but please make sure they don't add any pepper to it," Bobbie began. "And I'd like the salmon spinach salad, but instead of spinach, may I have romaine?"

The young, female server smiled indulgently. "Yes, of course."

"And the house dressing instead of the raspberry vinaigrette."

About an hour later, or so it felt to me, I got to order. "Fish tacos, just the way you make them."

"I'll have a glass of Prosecco," Bobbie said.

"Make it two," I said. Nothing like drinking in the middle of the day while enjoying good food and an amazing view.

When the server left, I brought up the subject of the poison in Courtney's drink. "I'm thinking the low dose might have been deliberate. Maybe he, or whoever hired him, wanted to make Courtney sick, not kill her."

"But why? If he wanted to make her sick, he could have used something less lethal."

I'd come up with a theory about that. "I think they wanted to send a message. Like a death threat."

Bobbie's eyes widened. "Do you really think so? Don't people usually deliver threats in person? Or if they want to stay anonymous, paste cut-up magazine letters onto a paper and leave it under your door?"

"I don't think that's how it's done these days." I paused while the server placed our drinks on the table and waited for her to leave.

"So how is it done?" Bobbie asked.

I shrugged. "I have no idea. But from what Courtney said, somebody who wants to buy the hotel has been making thinly veiled threats. Maybe they wanted to let Bat know they were serious."

"And nothing says serious like strychnine."

"Exactly."

Bobbie gave my theory some thought. "You might be on to something. We need to go to Hotel Elegance and talk to your boss."

"I'll do it tomorrow." I ignored the disappointed look on her face, but I wanted to see what else I could find out before I confronted Bat with my theories.

Besides, I wasn't going to my workplace on my day off. Only people who didn't have a life did that.

Chapter Ten

The next afternoon when I arrived at the hotel, Bat took off and didn't return until after the dinner crowd left. Dolph sat at one end of the bar while a couple at the other end groped each other. I made a gagging face which Dolph found entertaining, but Bat told me to take the rest of the night off. Even if it was a slow night, I would have thought he'd want me around for entertainment.

Remembering my promise to my grandmother to see what I could find out from Bat, I removed my vest and apron and sat down by Dolph, leaving a seat in between us. I didn't want him to get the wrong idea.

The couple got up to leave, and the woman smirked, as if to say she was getting some tonight and I wasn't. I pointed to Bat and grinned, hoping she'd get the wrong idea.

Bat leaned one strong arm on the bar. "Don't you have anywhere to go?"

He wasn't getting rid of me that easily, at least not tonight. "I want one of those free drinks you promised me when you hired me. Why don't you show me what you've got?"

Bat's flirtatious smile gave me tingles all over. "You're on, Whit."

I liked the way he said my name, like we were friends. I reminded myself he was my boss, not my friend. Then I reminded myself I didn't want him to be my friend anyway. He was so yummy.

"Here you go," he said, ripping me back to the real world. "An Elegance Sidecar."

He placed a honey-colored cocktail with a sugared rim in front of me. "I try to avoid sugar. It's not healthy."

"But alcohol is?"

"Point taken." I took a sip. "Oh, my. You really know how to make a girl happy." Why did double entendres fly out of my mouth every time Bat was within earshot?

Bat looked extremely self-satisfied. I'd seen that look before, and it gave me more tingles and a burning desire to run for the hills. If he wasn't engaged, the little angel on my shoulder would have her work cut out for her. I decided to steer the conversation toward less intimate subjects.

"So..." I began, "why are you selling the hotel?"

His smile evaporated. "I just want to do something else with my life instead of spending all my time here."

"That wasn't convincing at all," I said. "You need to work on your delivery." When he didn't react, I went on. "What else do you want to do with your life?"

Bat did that squinty thing he did when I first met him. He knew I saw right through him, but he wouldn't admit it. "Travel."

"Yeah, right." I took a big sip of the Sidecar before getting personal again. "Does this have anything to do with someone trying to poison Courtney?"

"No," he said defensively, followed by, "How do you know about that?"

I figured I'd protect my sources, namely the blabbermouth detective. "I took a sample of the drink and had it tested myself. Funny how someone went to the bother of putting poison in her drink but didn't put enough in it to kill her. Isn't that funny?"

"No, it's not." He started wiping down the bar moving farther away as he did. Then he washed glasses that were already clean. Pretty much anything he could do that wasn't talking with me.

I took the hint, downed the last of my drink, and headed home.

The next morning, Bobbie greeted me with, "Now where did I leave my phone?"

I grunted in response. Surely, she didn't expect an answer from me before I had my first cup of coffee.

She sighed. "I miss phones that stayed put so you always knew where to find them."

The freedom of walking around all day without a phone in your pocket or purse was a foreign concept to me. The thought terrified me. To speed up the process, I dialed her phone and soon heard a faint muffled ring coming from the living room. She retrieved her phone from between the sofa cushions.

"There's a message from Darla." Bobbie listened to the voice message, then called her friend. Pleasantries were exchanged.

While I waited for her to ask Darla about the license plate, I fixed myself a bowl of cereal and listened to Bobbie's side of the conversation.

"He said that?" Bobbie said into the phone. "I know you don't care if he gets fired, but he might. It might not look good on his job record, even if he doesn't choose to pursue a career in government clerical administration."

I gave her a hurry-up gesture followed by a well-what-did-she-say gesture, and she responded with a get-me-pen-and-paper gesture. She made some notes and hung up.

"Well?" I asked.

"The car is registered to a corporation, D and Q Holdings, Inc." Bobbie looked at her notes. "Her grandson wouldn't give her their address, but he did say they're located in Solana Beach."

"Great!" I grabbed the paper from her and opened my laptop to look them up.

An hour later I pried my eyes from the screen and rubbed my temples. "Are there any aspirin in this house?" Before she could answer my first question, I asked another. "Do you know where the Cook Islands are?"

"What an odd thing to ask." Bobbie scurried to the bathroom, returning with a pill bottle and a glass of water. "The Cook Islands are in the South Pacific. Why?"

"D and Q Holdings is, not surprisingly, a holding company. They own a bunch of companies, including DTL Capital Partners, LLC, which they list as a real estate investment company. But they're incorporated in the Cook Islands. Listen to this."

I read from the laptop screen. "There is no public registry, and information can be obtained only with permission from the Company itself."

"That doesn't seem right," Bobbie said. "You can't tell who the owner is?"

"Give me a chance." Frustration might have slipped into my voice.

"No need to snap at me," Bobbie said curtly.

"Sorry. I think I need a snack." I glanced at the clock. "Or lunch. When did it get to be so late?"

Bobbie made a couple of ham sandwiches with extra mayo, just the way I liked them. After wolfing down mine, I returned to my research. Another hour later, as I was ready to give up, I found some information I hoped would be helpful.

"I found the directors, or I should say director, since they only list one. Roy Brown."

"Is that even a real name?" Bobbie asked.

"I've got an address." I jumped to my feet. "I'm going to see what I can find out about Mr. Roy Brown."

"I'm coming with you," she said, heaving her purse over her shoulder.

I considered the wisdom of taking my grandmother into what could be a dangerous situation, weighed it against the even bigger headache I'd surely get if I argued with her, and made my decision.

I grabbed my car keys. "Let's go."

Chapter Eleven

Bobbie and I stood on the sidewalk in front of the Mail Drop Plus storefront. If I'd spent five more minutes on the internet, I would have realized Roy Brown's address was a post office box before making the drive.

"That's anticlimactic," I said. "Now, what do we do?"

"We go in, of course." She pushed through the doors into the austere, utilitarian interior with rows of mailboxes lining one wall.

I followed her to the counter where a clean-cut young man stood waiting to greet us. He looked very spiffy in a bright blue polo shirt with the company logo and matching ball cap.

"May I—" he began.

I interrupted him and got right to the point.

"We're looking for Roy Brown. He has a mailbox here. Number 347."

Bobbie nudged me in the ribs. "I apologize for my granddaughter's lack of manners. My name is Barbara Brown, and this is my granddaughter," she paused, then finished with, "Winona."

I raised my eyebrows but said nothing. I'd wait until later to ask why we'd gone incognito and why we hadn't come up with a better cover story in advance. Although she did deserve points for quick thinking.

"Nice to meet you, Mrs. Brown," the clerk said. After a quick glare aimed at me, he turned back to my grandmother and resumed smiling.

"Please call me Barbara," she said. "I'm so worried about Roy." She paused for dramatic tension. "He's my nephew, you see. I've been calling and calling, but he hasn't returned any of my calls or texts. He gave me this address to send his birthday card last April. I didn't realize it was a postal box." She heaved a wistful sigh. "I just don't know what to think."

The employee regarded her kindly. "I'm so sorry, Barbara, but due to the Mail Drop Plus policy, I can't give out any personal information about one of our customers."

"I understand," she said in a very understanding voice. "I wouldn't want to get you in any trouble." Another sigh. "I suppose you can't tell me if he's been in recently to pick up his mail." And a pause. "It's just that I'm so worried about him."

"I'm so sorry," he repeated, nodding sympathetically.

It was my turn for some acting. "Never mind, Grandma. Uncle Roy doesn't want to talk to you. It's better if you face facts."

Bobbie's eyes began to tear up. "But what if I never get a chance to apologize?" She turned back to the clerk. "I said some things I shouldn't have in the heat of the moment. I didn't mean them, really. I just want to say I'm sorry...while I still can."

I figured she'd get more information without me in the way. I patted her arm in what I hoped looked like a loving gesture. "I'll wait for you in the car."

As soon as I stepped outside, I chuckled at my grandmother's performance. The clerk seemed to buy the act, and hopefully she'd get something useful out of him.

I climbed into the car and turned on the radio. I'd just begun to groove to some old-school R&B when Bobbie opened the passenger door and got in.

Her grin gave her away. "It worked like a charm. You know what? I think we should apply to the CIA. We'd make great spies."

"When you're done patting yourself on the back, would you mind telling me what you found out?"

"Roy Brown collects his mail several times a week, always right around five o'clock."

"That's great! Wait. We don't even know what he looks like." I gave her a questioning look. "Do we?"

"I told the nice young man I hadn't seen him in years and asked if he still had a beard," she said, rightly proud of herself. "He's clean-shaven with short hair and drives a black Mercedes."

I whistled. "No way. I wonder if it's the same car that picked up our poisoner." Mercedes were more common than spray tans in this town, but maybe we'd gotten lucky.

"Only one way to find out. Stakeout!"

Bobbie was enjoying this a little too much. "It's only three o'clock. What should we do for the next two hours?"

"Let's get something to eat."

"We just ate," I reminded her.

"Then you can get an iced tea or mineral water or whatever. I want a snack. Casey's Corner Cafe has cherry pie to die for."

"Fine." I wouldn't say no to a piece of pie.

Casey's Corner was a short drive like everything in town. We both ordered cherry pie ala mode, and I asked the server for a double cappuccino hoping to prevent the inevitable post-pie coma. When our desserts arrived, they didn't disappoint.

"This is the flakiest crust I've ever had," I said

between bites. "Other than your homemade pie of course."

"Kiss up," she said, but her smile told me she appreciated the compliment. She was rightfully proud of her baking skills.

"What are we going to do if Roy Brown shows up for his mail today? It's probably not smart to confront him."

"Do you think he's the getaway driver you saw pick up the lowlife you chased?"

I considered her question. "Yeah, I do."

"Do you think he's behind Courtney's attempted poisoning?"

I thought that over for a bit. "I have a feeling they're both working for someone."

"Who?"

"Whoever is trying to buy Hotel Elegance. Probably the same people who just bought the Sandpiper. They're closing it down—I suspect they're planning to tear both hotels down and build some monster luxury condo complex. Ugh."

"So how do we find out who these people are?"

It occurred to me I could have been researching that question instead of stuffing my face with pie. "I'll see what I can find out later." I glanced at the pie-shaped clock on the wall. "We need to get going if we want to see if Roy Brown is gonna show today."

Fifteen minutes later, we parked in front of the Mail Drop Plus with plenty of time to spare.

"I'll need to get a thermos," Bobbie said.

I didn't want to ask, but I couldn't help myself. "Why do you need a thermos?"

"For stakeouts."

"This isn't going to become a regular thing, you know," I informed her.

"I don't know about that. Maybe I'll start up my own detective agency. I think I'd be an excellent investigator."

I turned my gaze upward. "Heaven help me."

She smacked my leg. "He's not going to listen to you. When was the last time you went to church?"

"Um, Easter?" I guessed. "I've been busy. Besides—"

"Look." She pointed excitedly at a car pulling up in front of us. "A black Mercedes. I don't have my distance glasses. Can you read the plates?"

"Ding-ding-ding. Congratulations. It's a winner."

"What do we do now?" Bobbie asked, one hand on the door handle. "Confront him?"

"We wait for him to get his mail and come back out."

"And then we confront him?" Bobbie asked eagerly.

"Then we follow him."

Chapter Twelve

My heart pounded in anticipation as we waited. If I could find out who Roy Brown worked for, I had a feeling all the pieces would fall into place. I tapped the steering wheel impatiently.

"Do you have an extra pair of sunglasses?" Bobbie asked. "It's so bright in this town. Don't you get tired of all the sunshine?"

I shot her a glance silently conveying my doubts about her judgement. "Come back for May gray or June gloom. Sounds like you'd love it."

"There he is," Bobbie whispered the moment Roy Brown emerged onto the sidewalk, as if I couldn't see him with my own eyes.

The sedan pulled out onto Coast Highway, and I followed. With all the traffic, I didn't need to worry about him noticing my car, but when he turned off the main road, I kept my distance. After driving two short blocks, he pulled into the City Hall parking lot. I found a spot two rows away.

"What's he doing here?" I wondered aloud. "It's five o'clock. Everything's got to be closing, right?"

"City council meeting," Bobbie said, opening her door. "I bet that's where he's going."

I reached for her arm to stop her. "Wait a sec. I don't want him to see us."

From inside the car, we watched Roy Brown climb the steps and slip through the doors along with several other people.

"Let's go." I motioned for Bobbie to follow me, my senses on hyper-alert. At the top of the steps, I pushed open the heavy wooden door, stepping inside with Bobbie close behind. The scent of aged wood and old varnish filled my nostrils. Dust particles danced in streams of sunlight filtering in from high windows.

As the door closed behind me, I blinked in the dim light and peered around the lobby searching for a sign of Roy Brown.

"There he goes," Bobbie whispered, pointing to her left where a pair of doors swung closed. A sign overhead said "City Council Chambers" in big bold letters.

The sound of my boots echoed through the empty lobby as Bobbie and I headed for the chambers.

"You really need some stealthier shoes." Bobbie pointed to her rainbow high-top sneakers. "Like mine."

Not bothering to dignify her comment with a response, I pushed the door open a crack and peeked inside. Several stern-faced men and women sat at a wide dais at the front of the room.

Bobbie nudged me from behind, and I stepped inside, doing my best to be unobtrusive. She followed me as I slipped into a seat in the last row.

All the city council seats were filled except for the one in the middle. A fifty-ish man with thinning gray hair and a dignified aura entered from the back and took the empty seat. He banged his gavel, welcomed the attendees, and asked that all cell phones be silenced.

Bobbie leaned over to whisper in my ear. "That's Mayor Aldridge."

An opening prayer was followed by the pledge of allegiance, roll call, and approval of the minutes. Next came several resolutions including one recognizing the local high school's girls' volleyball team for winning the state championship, which passed, and another, mandating "wacky hat Fridays," which did not.

It went downhill from there, as there were readings, recommendations, and votes pertaining to every facet of city business. I'd finally found something more boring than traffic school. I may have dozed off toward the end.

Bobbie elbowed me and hissed in my ear, "He's leaving."

We merged with the thirty or forty people who had suffered through the meeting with us as they left the chambers. Back in the lobby, I scoured the crowd for our guy.

Bobbie pointed at him walking down a long hall. "There he is."

"Shh," I cautioned "He'll see us if we go in that direction." Everyone else headed for the front doors. I didn't blame them.

Bobbie pointed to a sign for the ladies' room before heading in that direction.

When we reached the restroom, she said loudly, "No, no. I don't need to use the facilities. I'll wait for you right here."

I gave her a look to say, "What the heck do you think you're doing?" but she shooed me toward the door. I stepped inside, holding the door open slightly, hoping to hear what went on.

After a few minutes, my impatience grew, and I tried to get her attention. "Psst."

She took a step closer to me and whispered, "He's talking to one of the council members."

"What about?" I whispered back.

"I can't hear what they're saying. I'll have to get closer."

As loudly as I dared, I hissed, "No!" but she

ignored me. I leaned out of the door and watched as she walked past Roy and the councilman.

"Ma'am," the councilman said, "the offices are all closed."

"Oh, are they?" She sounded as innocent as any dotty old lady. "You're on the council, aren't you?"

Before the councilman could answer, Roy Brown said, "We'll finish this up later, as long as we're on the same page."

The councilman nodded and watched Roy walk to the door, not taking his eyes off him until he was out of sight. He seemed surprised to find my grandmother still waiting for his attention. "May I help you in some way?"

"Yes," she said. "You might at that. I'm very interested in historic preservation you see, and I'm wondering about the status regarding Hotel Elegance. There seems to be a holdup with the historic designation. Would you know what's causing the delay?"

Even from where I stood, I could sense the councilman's discomfort as he avoided making eye contact with Bobbie. "Their application was incomplete. We've sent them several notices, but we can't move ahead on an incomplete application."

"No, of course you can't," Bobbie agreed. "Perhaps you could explain to me the missing information that is required, and I can pass the information on to the owners."

"I'm afraid the deadline for resubmitting the application has passed."

"It has?" Bobbie sounded incredulous, and I didn't blame her. "But surely there's something that can be done. The hotel is a part of the town's history. Did you know Greta Garbo once stayed there?"

"Rules are rules," he said firmly. "Without them, there'd be chaos."

"Chaos? Since when is saving part of our fine city's history chaos? There's no way the owner of Hotel Elegance missed a single deadline."

The councilman's body stiffened in indignation. "And I'm telling you they did. What are you implying?"

Before she had a chance to answer him, I appeared at her side doing my best to appear nonchalant. "Let's go, Grandma. Time to get you home."

When we stepped back outside, the sun had sunk low in the sky and cast long shadows on the parking lot. I took a deep breath to get the stale city hall air out of my lungs. "What was that all about? Bat never said his application was incomplete or mentioned missing any deadline."

"I'd say there are some shady dealings going on with Roy Brown and that councilman. Was it just me, or did he seem as nervous as a mouse in a snake cage?"

"It wasn't just you."

We'd reached the bottom step when the black

sedan drove past. Roy Brown, in the driver's seat, looked right at us.

"How stupid of me." I took off toward the car.

"Slow down." Bobbie yelled as she hurried to keep up.

Instead, I ran faster. When I reached my car, I took a flying leap and slid across the hood to the driver's side, a stunt I'd learned early on in my career. Not only was it efficient, but it looked cool.

By the time Bobbie reached the car, I had the engine revved and in gear.

"Get in," I yelled, and pealed out of the parking spot the moment she slammed the door. "If Roy Brown was the one driving the car that picked up that creep, he probably recognized me."

"So?" She held onto the armrest as we hit a speed bump.

"I'm the one person who can connect the guy who tried to poison Courtney with him."

Bobbie struggled with her seat belt until it clicked. "And I suppose that's bad."

"Yes," I said. "That's bad."

We bounced onto the street, and I made a right turn, tires squealing. I had no idea which way Roy Brown had turned, but I soon had to admit I'd lost him.

"Darn." I would have used stronger language, but I didn't want to risk a lecture from Bobbie. I pulled over and threw the gearshift into park and took a deep breath in and out to help regain my sense of calm.

"You did your best, dear," Bobbie said. "I'm not sure what we could have done if we caught up with him anyway."

"Good point. I guess I wasn't thinking that far ahead." I put the car back in drive and pulled back into traffic. "I'll taking you home and then go talk to Bat."

"You're not taking me home."

"I'm the one driving, remember?" I could be just as stubborn as her, maybe more so, although she'd had more practice.

She crossed her arms, and I could feel her eyes boring into the side of my head. "I suppose you're going to yank me out of the passenger seat and throw me on the front yard? What will the neighbors think?"

I sighed, accepting defeat. "Fine." I made a u-turn.

Bobbie and I said hello to Courtney as we walked through the lobby to the elevator. We took seats at the end of the bar away from the tables. It was quieter, and we had less chance of being overheard.

Bat finished making a martini for one of the regulars then strolled over giving Bobbie a polite nod. "Are you joining us for dinner?"

Bobbie smiled up at him. "That's not a bad idea, although we did just have pie, so I'm not sure how hungry I am."

I shook my head. "We're not here to eat. We came to talk to you." I filled Bat in on what we'd learned about Roy Brown and how we followed him to city hall.

"You did what?" Bat looked first at me and then Bobbie. "You need to stay out of it. This isn't child's play. Someone could get hurt." He pointed at me. "You should know better than to involve your grandmother in some crazy stunt." He turned his attention to Bobbie. "And I should think you were old enough to know better."

"Why didn't you tell me your application was incomplete?" I asked him.

"What are you talking about?"

"The city councilman said so. That's what's held it up."

"That's great." Bat smiled for the first time since we'd arrived. "Then I can fix it and—"

"Hold on." I wanted to stop him before he got his hopes up. "He also said the deadline has passed."

"Also," Bobbie added, "he said you've been notified several times."

He looked confused. "But I've been calling two or three times every week, and they never told me any of this." He rubbed his forehead in frustration. "Bureaucracy."

"Crooked politicians and bribes, more like it," I said.

The look on Bat's face told me he'd known this before I said it. "Without proof, there's not much I can do."

"We can look into it and see if we can find a loophole."

"By Friday?"

"What happens Friday?"

"I sign the purchase agreement agreeing to sell them the hotel."

"Why would you do that?" I asked, but Bat's expression told me he didn't feel he had a choice. He'd do anything to protect his sister. I sighed. "That doesn't give us much time."

Bat pulled up a chair and sat next to Bobbie. For the first time I noticed the bags under his eyes. He lowered his voice to just above a whisper. "I don't want either of you getting involved. Trust me, you don't want to mess with these people."

"But if they've threatened you..."

"That's just it. They haven't. Not in so many words. I thought I could handle it until they tried to poison my little sister." He stared at me with his deep blue eyes, and I almost forgot what we were talking about until he said, "Promise me you'll stay out of it."

"But what if we can help?"

"Promise me." His voice, now stern and louder, told me it would be useless to argue.

After a long pause, I figured we could go back and

forth forever. I had better things to do. "Fine, I promise."

The moment we stepped inside the elevator and the doors closed, Bobbie said, "I didn't promise."

I gave her a shrug. "I had my fingers crossed."

Chapter Thirteen

The next night, I tended bar, staying out of Bat's way as much as possible after the third time he snapped at me. I can take a hint. Eventually.

Courtney took her usual spot at the end of the bar but spoke only in monosyllables. Once she'd finished her Black Daiquiri, she seemed to chill out. She switched to mineral water, which meant her mood stalled out at medium-level morose.

For some reason, I decided to try to cheer her up. I guess I like a challenge.

"Want to come watch me do free running this weekend?" I asked.

"I thought you didn't like people watching you."

"Normally, that's true," I said. "But I'm trying out some new tricks, and I'd like some feedback."

"What? None of your other friends are available?" There was a definite tone of sarcasm in her voice I hadn't heard before.

"What is with you and Bat today? Did someone hit you both with a grumpy stick?"

Instead of answering, Courtney picked up her purse and headed for the stairs. "See you later."

It was probably for the best. She had been starting to bring out my maternal instinct, and that needed to be shut down fast. It was bad enough I had a dog to look after.

As I wiped down the bar, a forty-ish man approached wearing an expensive suit. I'd put its price tag at three thousand, easy. He should have budgeted for a stylist to help him get rid of the east coast mobster vibe he exuded. I waited for him to take a stool, but he didn't seem to be in a hurry to sit down.

"I'm here to see Bat Keller," he announced.

"And you are?"

"None of your business." He took his phone out and snapped a picture of me.

"Hey!" I blinked from the flash. "What did you do that for?"

His smile was something between an evil grin and a sneer. "I wanted something to remember this moment by." He typed something on his phone, no doubt sending my picture to one of his cohorts.

I pulled out my phone and snapped a picture of

him before I went to look for Bat. "There's this creepy-looking guy asking for you."

"Slicked-back hair, expensive suit?" he asked.

"That's him."

"But it's only Wednesday." He peered around the corner, and then gave me a stern look. "Stay out of the way while I'm talking to him."

I followed Bat back to the bar. They moved to a nearby table, and I busied myself washing glasses. Luckily, I have excellent hearing, and I caught most of their conversation.

"But you said I have until Friday," Bat told the man.

"That was before your lady friend got involved."

"My lady friend?" Bat sounded confused. "You mean Whit? What's she got to do with it?"

"Never mind," the man said. "I'll be back tomorrow at four with the papers and my lawyer. Make sure she's not around."

I watched Greasy Hair push the elevator button. As soon as he stepped inside, Bat told me to keep an eye on the place until he got back.

Jenny appeared at the service bar. "Where'd Bat go now?"

"Not sure." I glanced at the order screen and poured two glasses of the house cabernet. "Hey, Jenny. What would you do if you couldn't work here?"

Her face fell. "So, he is selling the hotel? Is it a done deal?"

"No, not at all," I lied. "Bat would never sell this place." Not willingly, that was for sure. "I was just curious if, I don't know, maybe you wanted to go back to college or start a business."

"Doing what?"

"Never mind." I set the glasses on her tray, but she didn't pick it up. She stared over my shoulder, lost in thought. I turned to see what she was looking at, but all I saw was the ocean and some fluffy white clouds.

"I'd love to go back to school someday, after the kids are out of the house. When you're a single mother, you don't spend a lot of time thinking about your own future. It's pretty much just getting through to the next day, you know?"

I nodded, although I didn't know. Not really. Sure, I was broke, but when you're living at your parents' beach house, it's not quite the same thing.

I'd finished neatly lining up all the bottles on the shelf behind the bar when Bat returned and handed me an envelope. "Turns out I don't need your services any longer."

Peeking in the envelope, I saw a stack of cash. "I'm being fired?"

"Let go."

"Oh good, that's much better than being fired." I

felt an unpleasant sensation in my stomach. "Maybe I can help."

"You've helped enough," he said. "I've paid you through the weekend, but you can leave now."

"I can stay if you want to talk. I've heard it helped sometimes." I really wanted to help.

"What I want is for you to leave."

"Fine." I took off my apron and vest and tossed them on the bar and headed for the stairs. When I reached the lobby, the reception desk was empty. Courtney must have gone home for the night.

This wasn't my fault, I told myself. This was Greasy Hair and his cronies' fault. And a certain crooked city councilman.

But what could I do about it in less than twenty-four hours?

Chapter Fourteen

I plopped down on the sofa next to Bobbie and told her about my crappy evening, including the part about getting fired. Kit climbed over Bobbie's lap to give me a lick on the neck.

"Ick." I put the dog down, but she jumped right back up and nipped my ear. "Ow."

"She wants to play. If you would pet her, she'd calm down." Bobbie's suggestion implied I knew nothing about caring for a pet. She was right.

"Fine." I stroked her with one hand while I checked my social media accounts. Two of my former coworkers had started filming a new superhero movie, so I knew there were jobs. My emails told a different story. "I'm sorry, Whit," my former stunt coordinator wrote. "There's not much work right now, but I'll keep you in mind."

Bobbie stood, and Kit jumped onto the floor, wagging her tail. "Can I get you something while I'm up?" She headed for the kitchen, the dog on her heels.

"Yeah," I said, "the key to the liquor cabinet."

Once I had access to the hard stuff and a selection of liqueurs, I lined up the martini glasses. First, I made us two Black Daiquiris, which Bobbie declared were delicious.

Next, I tried my hand at a couple of Old Fashioneds. Bobbie quit on me after the Aviations.

"Lightweight," I muttered, sprawling on the sofa with my gin and tonic. "Bartenders can get work anywhere, right?"

"There are worse things to do for a living," Bobbie said. "Of course, you could always marry for money. It worked out well in my case."

"You're not fooling me." I overenunciated my words in an attempt to hide my inebriated status. "You married for love. Grandpa just happened to be rich."

"He was a mighty good man, and I will miss him until the day I die." Her sweet and sad expression was the last thing I remembered until I woke up the next morning. How I made it to my bed I had no idea.

I shuffled out to the patio, hoping some fresh air would revive me. Bobbie followed me with a glass of tomato juice. "Drink this."

"Stop yelling." I took the glass and gulped. I nearly spit it out. "What the heck is in that?"

"Just drink it. You'll feel better."

I gave her the best evil look my puffy eyes could manage but complied. Her hangover remedies were legendary.

Bobbie sat in the chair next to me and leaned forward. "I've been up for hours thinking about how we can help Bat and Courtney keep the hotel, and I made a few calls this morning."

"Bat doesn't want our help."

"Too bad." She waved a dismissive hand. "He's getting it whether he wants it or not. The scuttlebutt is that there's some company quietly trying to buy up properties so they can build high-rise resorts. The locals aren't too happy about it."

"Yeah? What's that got to do with us?"

Bobbie raised an eyebrow. "If Bat's hotel is registered as a historic landmark, then it can't be torn down. If that's the case, I'm guessing the company won't want it."

"I figured out that much." I held my nose and gulped down the rest of the tomato elixir. "I still don't see what we can do about it."

After staring at me for several seconds, Bobbie went back indoors, returning shortly with a cup of steaming coffee heavy on the cream. I took a sip and started to feel twenty percent awake.

She took a seat across from me. "You're planning to do nothing, then? Let Bat and Courtney lose the hotel that's been in their family for nearly a century?"

"Number one." I held up my index finger. "There's nothing we can do. Number two." I held up the second finger. "Bat told me to keep out of it. He fired me, remember?"

"I never realized you were such a quitter," Bobbie mumbled.

Now I was fifty percent awake. "What did you say?"

"Good. I've got your attention. I suggest you listen to someone older and, hopefully, wiser. You will regret it for a long time if you don't help your friends save their hotel."

"They're not my friends." I stood up and crossed my arms. "Bat is, or was, my boss—nothing more."

"And Courtney?" Bobbie asked.

"Courtney needs to grow up and learn to take care of herself. I can't be responsible for her. I'm not doing that great a job just taking care of myself, in case you haven't noticed."

"I don't think that's true at all. You've had an amazing career. There've been setbacks, sure, but you've come back stronger every single time."

I didn't feel particularly strong at that moment, but she did have a point.

Bobbie kept talking. "We'll talk about how you're

afraid to get close to people because you don't want to get hurt later."

"No thanks." I'd get a therapist if I wanted to dig into the deep, dark crevices of my psyche. Which I didn't. "Why is helping Bat and Courtney so important to you? You hardly know them."

She grinned. "No, but you do. And you care about them. Besides, what else do we have planned?"

One look at her satisfied, determined face, and I knew she wouldn't be dissuaded. And she was right. I couldn't let Bat and Courtney down. "Fine. Let's go save Hotel Elegance."

It was already ten a.m., which didn't give us a lot of time—less than six hours. I got dressed in my typical black t-shirt and jeans and joined my grandmother in the living room to strategize.

"Do you remember your Uncle Chuck?" Bobbie asked. "He was related only by marriage, and when he divorced your aunt, the rest of the family disowned him. But I liked him, so I've always kept in touch."

"I think I remember him," I said, wondering why she was bringing him up now. "Short guy with curly hair?"

She nodded. "He plays golf with the mayor, not to mention he's one of the biggest donors to his reelection campaign. While you were dillydallying, I called him, and he's going to see if he can arrange a meeting."

"Why would Uncle Chuck, who's not even really an uncle, go out of his way for us?"

She gave me one of her sweetest smiles. "Uncle Chuck had an indiscretion a few years back that he'd rather keep from the public, not to mention his wife. I didn't want to bring it up, but desperate times, as they say."

"Call for desperate measures," I said, completing the phrase.

Her phone rang, and she answered "Hello, Chuck. Yes, we're free for lunch. Of course, I know where it is. We'll see you at one."

"One o'clock doesn't give us much time," I said. "I think we should go back to the police station. We can tell them Roy Brown was involved in Courtney's poisoning. They could bring him in for questioning."

"But we don't have any proof," Bobbie said.

I shrugged. "The police can't expect us to do all their work for them." I tried to connect the pieces in my mind. "Roy Brown is the director for DTL Capital Partners. There must be a connection between DTL and slick-haired guy."

"You don't know his name?"

"Give me a sec." I pulled out my laptop to find out who had bought the Sandpiper Inn. I found a press release from the previous month. "It says here that Donoland Resorts purchased the hotel next door."

"Donoland? That's interesting."

"Why? Have you heard of them?"

Bobbie shrugged noncommittally. "Just in passing."

I considered digging deeper, but we had only a few hours left before Bat would no longer be the owner of Hotel Elegance. I felt sad thinking of the hotel being reduced to rubble.

It didn't take long to find out the CEO of Donoland was a man named Jordan Anderson, and after more digging, I found a picture of him. I compared it to the picture I'd taken with my phone.

"He's our guy," I announced. "Donoland must be connected to DTL in some way. Or maybe they share resources. Like thugs." If I had another hour or two for research, I had no doubt I could uncover the connection. But I didn't have that time. I closed my laptop. "We'd better get going."

◆ ❯ ❯

I'd never been to Mersea, since lunch there would set me back more than my car payment.

Uncle Chuck introduced me to the mayor. Mayor Aldridge, formally attired in a nicely tailored off-the-rack suit, shook my hand firmly, then turned to Bobbie.

"Such a pleasure to see you again, Mrs. Leland." He exuded warmth and sincerity, which made me suspicious.

Uncle Chuck, casually dapper in a Ralph Lauren polo shirt and khakis, had hardly changed at all since I'd last seen him. He held out a chair for Bobbie, while I claimed the seat next to her.

After we ordered drinks and got the small talk out of the way, Bobbie got to the point. "Mr. Mayor, we need an approval on the Hotel Elegance historical designation by this afternoon."

Chuck laughed. The mayor laughed. Bobbie and I did not laugh.

When he realized we were serious, the mayor said, "That's not possible."

"The owners of Hotel Elegance are being pushed around and threatened by some unsavory people, and I don't like it. My granddaughter," she gestured to me, "wants to go to the police about her suspicions of bribery and collusion. I think she's on the right track, but I convinced her to hold off until we spoke with you. You see, there's a connection to one of your city council members."

Chuck pulled his head back, turning his two chins into three. "I had no idea they were planning to make these sorts of accusations," he told the mayor. "I apologize for their outrageous behavior. They're not even really related to me," he added as an afterthought.

"I'm not interested in causing trouble," Bobbie continued, speaking in a soothing tone she might have used to calm a crying toddler. "I know you're an honest, ethical man, and you'll take care of the councilman in your own way. I don't want to interfere in city politics."

The mayor smiled tentatively. "I appreciate that. I will make sure it's handled."

"However," Bobbie went on, "my granddaughter doesn't have the same, shall we say, understanding of how government works. You see, the owners are being coerced into signing a contract to sell their hotel that has been in their family for generations."

"I'm very familiar with the hotel and the family," the mayor said. "But the historic designation—"

Bobbie interrupted him. "If the sale happens at four o'clock this afternoon, there's no telling what Whit might do."

The mayor glanced at me, and I countered with my best tough-lady glare.

"You and I both know that Hotel Elegance is of historic significance," Bobbie continued. "The paperwork is just a formality."

The mayor tugged at his collar. "I don't think you understand how these things work, Mrs. Leland."

Bobbie spoke slowly and clearly, making sure the mayor heard each word. "The local papers would have a field day with a story about government corruption and crooked real estate deals. I'd hate to have your good name dragged through the mud when you have nothing to do with it."

"Yes." The mayor nodded. "I see what you mean."

Bobbie picked up her purse and stood. "It sounds as though we understand each other."

The mayor stood also. "We do. Come to my office at three, and I will have the necessary paperwork if it is humanly possible."

I threw in my two cents. "You're the mayor. Of course, it's possible."

Bobbie reached out to shake his hand. "I'll be there at two-thirty."

Following Bobbie toward the restaurant's front door, I complained, "I didn't even get to eat lunch."

We stopped at the reception stand, where a woman handed Bobbie a bag. She handed it to me.

"What's this?" I asked.

"I called and ordered takeout before we arrived," Bobbie said. "This way, Uncle Chuck gets stuck with the bill, and we duck out early."

"I thought you liked Uncle Chuck."

"I do, but we are running out of time."

Chapter Fifteen

After eating our delicious seafood salads in the car, I dropped Bobbie off at the mayor's office. She insisted on meeting with him alone, and we arranged to rendezvous in front of the Hotel Elegance.

After parking on the street outside the hotel, I sat in my car checking the time on my phone every thirty seconds. With my anxiety mounting, I got out and paced in front of the hotel. The minutes ticked by relentlessly while I waited for my grandmother to arrive.

What was taking her so long?

I glanced at the time again. Just fifteen minutes to go before the four o'clock deadline. This was cutting it too close for comfort.

The greasy-haired bully I now knew as Jordan

Anderson had warned me to stay away, but I had to do something. I'd have to stall him somehow until Bobbie arrived. I entered the hotel lobby and made a beeline for the stairs to the roof. Courtney glanced up from her post, but quickly turned away.

A man stepped in front of me before I could reach the staircase.

"Well, well," I said. "If it isn't my old friend Roy Brown. Somehow, I'm not at all surprised to see you here."

"You're not going upstairs." He looked bigger standing in front of me than he had sitting in his car. Bigger and meaner. Even if my grandmother arrived in time, we'd never get past this goon. I began to lose hope.

"Oh, well, you can't blame a girl for trying." I turned as if to leave, then pivoted and headed straight for him. I darted to the left to fake him out, then swung around him on the right. Making a dash for the stairs, I gave it everything I had, but he grabbed my ankle, and I went face forward into the carpet. I knew how to fall, so I didn't hurt myself, but my pride was damaged.

Roy picked me up by the waist and carried me kicking like a wild dog out the front door where he deposited me on the sidewalk before slamming the door behind me. A few passersby stopped to stare, then kept walking.

Feeling weak and defeated, I picked myself up and dusted the dirt off my pants. Anger began to build inside me. How dare these creeps use their muscle and money to take advantage of two decent people like Bat and Courtney. They were about to lose everything, and here I was standing on the sidewalk like some powerless wimp. I was not powerless, and I was certainly not a wimp.

"I am Whitley Leland," I told myself, "And I am a badass woman. I come from a long line of badass women."

Then something hit me. Literally. One of those fancy drink umbrellas bounced off my head and landed on the pavement. I looked up to see a little girl leaning over the railing of the rooftop lounge laughing.

I laughed too. I waved my finger at her. "I'm going to get you for that," I said with a grin. To myself I added, "Here I come, Bat."

I'd done it before, just the other way around. Going up would be harder than coming down had been, but I had so much anger-fueled adrenaline, I felt like I could do anything. Backing up to get a head start, I ran and leaped for the awning but missed. On the second try, I caught the edge and swung on top.

Standing on the awning, it felt springy not unlike a trampoline. After five or six bounces I grabbed onto the third-floor balcony.

The girl squealed with delight. "Mommy, mommy! Spider Lady is coming."

From there, it was just a quick scamper up the drainpipe and onto the rooftop railing, where I stood and surveyed the scene. The girl's happy squeals began to attract the attention of the diners, including her mother who gasped when she saw me. Bat looked up from the table where he sat across from Jordan, a pen in his hand. His mouth dropped open when he saw me.

Jordan glared, not trying to hide his contempt before trying to regain control of the situation. "Just sign it," he hissed.

Bat laughed, incredulous. He called out to me, "Are you here to save the day?"

"I sure am."

"What do you think you're going to do?" Jordan stood and pulled his phone out his pocket. He yelled into it. "Get up here. Now!"

Bat called out to me. "Have you lost your mind?"

"That is a distinct possibility."

I looked over my shoulder at the street below and spotted Bobbie climbing out of a taxi. She gave out a tiny yelp when she saw me before hurrying to the hotel door.

Roy Brown appeared at the top of the stairs. "What the—? How did you—?"

"Hey, Roy." I did my best to sound casual as my heart pounded wildly in my chest.

He rushed over to me but couldn't figure out how to grab me without accidentally pushing me off.

"Get her off there," Jordan said. "I don't care which side of the railing she ends up on."

"That's okay. I'll come down." I climbed down from the railing, doing my best to buy time. "I just wanted to let Bat know he's about to have a visitor."

The elevator opened and Bobbie emerged waving papers in the air. "Hello, everyone. I hope I haven't kept you waiting."

"Who are you?" Jordan asked.

I strolled over to the bar. "Allow me to introduce you. Jordan Anderson, meet Roberta Leland, my grandmother. I think you'll find that what she has in her hands is the historic designation that you and Roy Brown here tried to keep my friends from obtaining."

"As usual," Bobbie said, "you are correct, dear. Of course, this isn't the original. That's on file with the city. But I thought you might like a copy." She held the papers out to Jordan, but he didn't reach for them, instead folding his arms and scowling. After a moment, she handed them to Bat instead.

Bat quickly perused the document, then looked Jordan in the eye. "Leave my property now, or I'll call the police."

Jordan's eyes narrowed, but he knew he'd been beaten.

As he and Roy headed for the stairs, I called out after him. "And don't come back, either of you."

My adrenaline still pumping, I pulled out two barstools, motioning to Bobbie to take one.

"I could use a drink," I said.

Bat grinned. "Two Black Daiquiris coming right up."

Chapter Sixteen

I invited Bat and Courtney over to watch the season finale of *Legends of the Defenders*. Courtney sat on the sofa between Bobbie and me with Kit curled up on her lap.

"Hey," I scolded Bat. "You're hogging the popcorn."

He laughed and handed me the bowl before going to the kitchen to retrieve the champagne bottle.

As he refilled my flute, I pointed to the screen. "There. That's me. Kicking butts and taking names."

"Awesome," Courtney said. "It looks just like Brit. I mean you look like her."

"That's the point," I said. "Watch this part." I got up from the sofa and did the moves along with TV me. The last scene was coming up where I jumped out the window.

"Whoa," Courtney said, her eyes wide. "Did you really jump out the window ten stories up?"

Bat carried the empty bottle back to the kitchen. "I don't know why you're surprised. You saw her jump off a three-story roof."

I grinned as a cork popped in the kitchen. "I jumped through the window, but it's not real glass. And it's not ten stories up. They filmed that part separately."

Bat returned with a fresh bottle and topped off our glasses. I returned to my spot on the sofa.

"I've never had such a cool friend," Courtney said.

I felt a funny twist in my stomach. "I've never had a hotel owner for a friend."

"Two hotel owners," Bat corrected. He looked into my eyes, and my insides went all mushy. "By the way, I'm sorry about firing you, and I take it back. You're one of the best bartenders I've ever had."

"Aw, heck. I would have fired me a whole lot sooner if I were you."

Bobbie, who'd been quiet all this time, spoke up. "She's available for another week or two, and then we're going to my house in Arrow Springs."

"We are?" I asked.

"I can take only so much sunshine. I miss home. I miss my friends." She reached over Courtney and patted me on the knee. "I talked to Angela, and she won't fight me if you come stay for the winter."

"Ugh." That one word summed it up for me. "Sorry, but I'm going to get back to L.A. ASAP."

"Yes, I know," Bobbie said. "But you can come stay for a little while, can't you?"

"Where is Arrow Springs?" Courtney asked. "Can I come visit sometime?"

"Of course," Bobbie said. "It's in the mountains just two or three hours away, depending on traffic, of course. You're both welcome."

"Arrow Springs," I said. "Where winter is actually winter, with snow and ice and scary icicles hanging off eaves waiting to stab you through the heart. What am I supposed to do with myself there? I hate the snow."

"Don't they have restaurants in Arrow Springs?" Bat asked.

"Very nice ones," Bobbie said. "We'll take you out to eat when you come visit."

"Maybe he doesn't want to come visit." I felt my cheeks flush.

"You can get a job as a bartender," Bat said. "I'll give you a reference."

"And during the day," Bobbie said. "You can help me start my private investigator business. I've signed up for classes, and I'll be opening an office in Arrow Springs as soon as I get my license."

Charlie, Bat, and I looked at her and together said, "What?"

Chapter Seventeen

Bobbie relaxed on the patio while I tried to stuff all my belongings into two suitcases. Giving up on that hopeless task, I went in the kitchen to retrieve a few shopping bags. The advantage of driving my own car up to Arrow Springs meant I could be a bit more flexible.

I stuck my head out the patio door. "You ready?"

"I've been ready." Bobbie's voice barely hid her impatience. She couldn't wait to get home to the mountain community where she'd lived since before I was born.

"I'll just take one more look around then and make sure we haven't forgotten anything." It was a ritual my mother had taught me whenever we left a hotel room. As a child, my job had been opening every drawer and closet door to make sure nothing got left behind.

The bathroom yielded a jar of very expensive face cream I was pretty sure my mother wouldn't miss. After a longing gaze at the liquor cabinet, I checked in with Bobbie again. "Do you have plenty of wine and liquor at your place?"

"Yes, plenty."

"You sure?"

"Yes." She paused. "Though I wouldn't be mad if a bottle of Dom made it into your suitcase. It's good to be prepared in case there's a reason to celebrate."

"I'll check." I liked her idea of what it meant to be prepared.

The last room on my sweep was the guestroom Bobbie had been using. I didn't find a single thing in any of the drawers or the closet. Satisfied, I took one last look around before we left the beach cottage. Who knew when we would return?

Something white lying on the floor between the nightstand and the bed caught my attention. Probably a receipt or a shopping list Bobbie had dropped.

As I got closer, I saw it was a small envelope. Picking it up, I read Bobbie's Arrow Springs address handwritten in cursive. It had been postmarked two months ago in Ohio. I unfolded the flap and slipped out a plain notecard. Holding my breath, I read my birth mother's neatly scrawled words.

Mom,

I can't do what you ask.

One day, when it's safe, I will see my daughter again. I don't expect her to forgive me, but I hope she can understand once I've told her everything.

Will she forgive you?

I stared at the signature, a name I knew well but had almost never heard spoken out loud.

Julia.

Thank you for reading *The Black Daiquiri, an Arrow Investigations Humorous, Action-Adventure Mystery!*

To learn about what happens when Whit, Bobbie and Kit arrive in Arrow Springs, order *Old Fashioned Murder*—available now at most retailers!

Get updates from KC Walker and the real-life Kit by signing up at kcwalkerauthor.com.

KC Walker also writes and publishes sweet cozy mysteries under the name Karen Sue Walker, including the Bridal Shop and Haunted Tearoom Mysteries. Visit karensuewalker.com to learn more.

By the way, I love hearing from readers—you can email me at kc@karensuewalker.com.

How to Make a Black Daiquiri

A Black Daiquiri is a traditional rum daiquiri with an added ingredient to make it appear nearly black.

Ingredients:

- 2 ounces light rum
- 1 ounce freshly squeezed lime juice
- ¾ ounce simple syrup
- Darkening agent (see note)

Steps:

1. Add rum, lime juice, and syrup to a shaker with ice. Shake until well chilled.

2. Add a small amount of darkening agent and mix. Add additional until desired color is reached.
3. Strain into a martini glass and garnish as desired.

Note: Activated charcoal is one darkening agent, but it should be used with caution. I chose to use Ebony Carrot Supercolor Powder (available on Amazon) which gives the drink a lovely dark purple color.

For more recipes, bonus content, and pictures of the real-life Kit, sign up at kcwalkerauthor.com.

Made in United States
North Haven, CT
06 August 2023

39994470R00093